Friends of the Library

"*Friends of the Library* is the book I have long hoped that someone would write—a beautifully wrought hymn of praise to readers and book-lovers in the most sacred of places, the libraries where we find both. Rich in character, keen insight and local color, this heartwarming collection celebrates the surprising power of story to bring us together."

—**Cassandra King**, author of the best-selling novels *The Sunday Wife* and *The Same Sweet Girls* and the upcoming memoir *Tell Me a Story*

"A love letter to big lives found in small southern towns, *Friends of the Library* reminds us of the affecting, empowering ways libraries serve as safe havens for the stories and storytellers in our communities. Susan Cushman deftly braids together a tapestry of connected lives on the cusp of discovery and change, each strengthened by their bonds to one another and brightly lit by the stalwart optimism of Adele Covington, a touring writer and graceful steward of good will. May all who enter these pages leave as friends."

—**Jonathan Haupt**, executive director of the Pat Conroy Literary Center and coeditor with Nicole Seitz of *Our Prince of Scribes: Writers Remember Pat Conroy*

"Susan Cushman's new book *Friends of the Library* ties the geography of community to the geography of the human heart and adds destiny's arrow, leading to a renewed romance, a published manuscript, hearts and diseases healed, and a home for the homeless. With a light hand Susan has touched on some of the most poignant moments and monumental challenges we face as individuals. What ties the stories together so beautifully is the truth that plays out in them: None of us are meant to make it through our lives alone and, we have the power to better the lives of those around us. I loved the sense of community reflected in the stories, the deep love for literature, and the compassion of the characters as they championed all that was good in the world down to the tiniest crumb of kindness. When I finished the book I immediately joined Friends of the Library in my own city. Obviously, I've been missing a lot of chances to be part of a great community of like-minded souls."

—**River Jordan**, Clearstory Radio host and author of *Praying for Strangers* and *Confessions of a Christian Mystic*

"Susan Cushman's latest book is clever and pioneering. She creates a collection of fiction stories that unmask real-world problems through an author's visit to Friends of the Library meetings, and then becomes a pivotal force in helping the characters resolve crises—cancer, homelessness, domestic violence, and much more. Another work by Susan Cushman I couldn't put down."

—**Niles Reddick**, Pulitzer Prize, PEN-Faulkner, and Pushcart Prize nominee, and author of *Reading the Coffee Grounds* and *Drifting Too Far From the Shore*

"Readers already know Susan Cushman as a talented novelist and nonfiction author. This time she uses short stories to take us on a fictional tour of Mississippi, giving us a delightful peek inside the 'Friends' library groups of ten real cities and towns. Anyone who knows the South and its quirky residents will love this entertaining and insightful collection of stories."

—**John Floyd**, Edgar Award nominee, three-time Derringer Award winner, and 2018 Edward D. Hoch Memorial Golden Derringer Award winner, a lifetime achievement award

"Susan Cushman has crafted a set of delightful short stories that will make everyone want to be an author visiting Friends of the Library groups like her main character Adele Covington, who finds herself involved in difficult problems in the lives of those coming to hear her talks. Adoption, domestic violence, homelessness, and other hard issues are addressed and resolved as Adele comes to care for those she meets along the way. I hope that as Susan continues to publish, she adds to these stories, creating an ongoing series."

—**Ellen Morris Prewitt**, editor of *Writing Our Way Home: A Group Journey Out of Homelessness*

"Susan Cushman takes us on an emotional journey, down Mississippi's back roads and up its express lanes, to libraries and the readers who love them, who revel in the camaraderie found in books. Ultimately, she weaves her own story into the fabric of those who seek understanding, solace, and redemption through their shared experiences. This book is a love letter to librarians, readers, and the characters who speak to them. Cushman's fiction is the catalyst that draws from them their individual, unique, and poignant stories."

—**Suzanne Hudson**, author of *All the Way to Memphis* (short stories)

"The world needs more of these delightful, heartwarming stories, which are well-drawn vignettes that follow narrator, author Adele Covington, to ten Mississippi author events hosted by Friends of the Library. We learn the landmarks and history of each town. We meet its citizens in each slice of life story that ranges from homelessness to domestic violence to cancer. If you've ever wanted a peek inside the life of a writer, *Friends of the Library* depicts a delightful author as she introduces her novel at library events and then adds more to the equation by illustrating how, when it comes to authors and readers, the gift of the relationship is mutually beneficial."

—**Claire Fullerton**, author of *Mourning Dove, Dancing to an Irish Reel* and *A Portal in Time*

"*Friends of the Library* is a love letter to southern readers and writers that also manages to tackle serious social issues. In a world of Twitter and twaddle, Susan Cushman gives us a timely reminder of the simple pleasures of your local library. Find this book and check it out!"

—**Jim Dees**, author of *The Statue and the Fury*, and host of the Thacker Mountain Radio Show

"Susan Cushman gives readers the grand tour of Mississippi, introducing us to recognizable characters and covering every topic from alcoholism to faith, domestic violence to Southern cooking. This book could only have been written by someone who loves our great state and who longs to celebrate both the writers and readers who call it home."

—**Julie Cantrell**, *New York Times* and *USA Today* bestselling author of *Into the Free*

"Who says happy endings no longer exist? Susan Cushman's *Friends of the Library* doesn't shy away from the ugliness of the world and the missteps we often take on our journeys through it, but redemption is always within reach. These stories provide hope in what can often seem like a hopeless world. Adele Covington, who stands at the center of each story, is an angel, and the people in the small towns of Mississippi won't soon forget her, nor will those who read this book."

—**Lee Martin**, author of *The Mutual UFO Network*

"Susan Cushman is bold, honest, witty, and, well, darn it, the woman can write. Her latest book, *Friends of the Library*, is a collection of short stories tying author Adele Covington to the Friends of the Library groups across Mississippi. Although Adele concentrates on her book tour, selling books becomes more about saving the people who come to hear her. And because Adele Covington cares, ten Mississippi towns will never be the same."

—**Richelle Putnam**, author of *Mississippi and the Great Depression*, Bronze Medal recipient, 2017 Foreword Indie Book Award; and *The Inspiring Life of Eudora Welty*, 2014 Moonbeam Children's Book Awards, Silver Medal recipient

Friends of the Library
by Susan Cushman

ISBN 978-1-63393-895-3

This is a work of fiction. The characters are both actual and fictitious. With the exception of verified historical events and persons, all incidents, descriptions, dialogue and opinions expressed are the products of the author's imagination and are not to be construed as real.

"Meridian: Gypsies, Orphans, and Ghosts" was previously published in *Deep South Magazine*, October 31 2018.

Published by

 köehlerbooks™

210 60th Street
Virginia Beach, VA 23451
800—435—4811
www.koehlerbooks.com

For Phyllis –
♡ Susan

FRIENDS

of the

LIBRARY

SHORT STORIES BY

Susan Cushman

Susan Cushman

VIRGINIA BEACH
CAPE CHARLES

For all the members of the Friends of the Library everywhere,
but especially those wonderful people in these towns in Mississippi who
invited me to come and share my books with you.
Thanks for inspiring these stories.

When you read a short story, you come out a little more aware and a little more in love with the world around you.

—*George Saunders*

Without libraries what have we? We have no past and no future.

—*Ray Bradbury*

ABOUT ME

Adele Covington

I was born and raised in Jackson, Mississippi, coming of age in the 1960s. As a child, I spent lots of time in Meridian with my grandmother and later attended the University of Mississippi in Oxford. Yet, other than the time I spent away at school, I never ventured into my state's many smaller unheralded towns—until my seventh decade.

By then, I had become an author, and I went on a book tour to speak to the Friends of the Library groups in ten small Mississippi towns. While I enjoyed speaking at famous bookstores and prestigious literary festivals and conferences all over the Southeast, I was also drawn to the humble library patrons and their quaint and quirky communities.

How could I not want to write about the people in towns with names like Eupora, Aberdeen, Senatobia, and Pontotoc? How could I forget the impression the folks made on me in West Point and Southaven, and the college towns of Oxford and Starkville? Or my experience at the Miss Mississippi pageant in Vicksburg? And learning about gypsies and ghosts in Meridian? What great settings for the important issues I wanted to explore through the venue of short stories: homelessness, alcoholism, domestic abuse, adoption, Alzheimer's, biracial relationships, cancer, childhood sexual abuse, eating disorders, kidnapping, and even ghosts.

But not to worry; even the darkest tales are lined with silver, and some stories are positively uplifting, with Mississippi blues and rock and roll, and a bit of late-life romance thrown in just for fun.

I join you, my readers, as more of an observer. At other times I engage in my characters' lives, participating in their journeys and being affected by my relationship with them. Why do they unbosom so easily to me? Maybe it's because of how candidly I share important aspects of my life when speaking with them at their Friends of the Library meetings. Maybe it's just my nature that invites their confidences.

Although the stories in this volume were inspired by library visits, I must admit that the characters in these stories and their experiences are fictional. Well, a couple of characters are real—like the well-known musicians who interact with small-town Mississippi characters, and the young woman who was crowned Miss Mississippi.

One more disclosure: I'm a fictional author. But never mind that for now.

THE STORIES

Eupora: *Francine and Odell*
•1•

Aberdeen: *Charlotte*
•15•

Oxford: *Avery*
•27•

Senatobia: *John and Mary Margaret*
•50•

Southaven: *Shelby*
•65•

Starkville: *Jeanne*
•81•

West Point: *Crystal*
•97•

Pontotoc: *Robert Earl*
•108•

Vicksburg: *Miss Mississippi*
•118•

Meridian: *Gypsies, Orphans, and Ghosts*
•126•

Acknowledgments and Disclosure
•134•

Discussion Guide
•137•

EUPORA

Francine and Odell

Eupora, Mississippi, harbors around 2,500 souls today living on 5.6 square miles of land. It is only sixty-five miles south of Oxford, but I never visited while attending the University of Mississippi. I had only heard of the town because my guidance counselor in high school was from Eupora. Some of the kids at our school teased him, saying that he was from a town with wooden sidewalks. Turns out they were right about the sidewalks.

Three Indian tribes fought over Eupora's geography in the 1700s, and it was finally settled in 1889 thanks largely to the Georgia Pacific Railroad. The railroad depot is the oldest building in Eupora, which was designated a historic district on the National Register in 2011. The Webster County Library was organized in the 1960s, and the town's budget is so small that they only employ a part-time librarian three days a week. But they boast several avid readers, including some retired school teachers, in the very active Webster County Friends of the Library group. Fourteen such devotees attended my reading.

The group is comprised mostly of women, but there was one man who arrived a few minutes after I started talking about my novel. He slipped in quietly and found a chair against the wall by the door instead of joining the ladies at either of the two long tables. Miss Eleanor—the woman who had been serving lunch just before he arrived—greeted the lone male with a pimento cheese sandwich and a small bag of chips on a paper plate. He nodded as he accepted the plate and immediately began to eat. His clothes were ragged and dirty, and his long hair and beard looked like they hadn't been washed in a while.

After I talked about my novel and spent a few minutes answering questions, I decided to turn the tables and ask a few—something I often do at book events.

"How many of you are retired school teachers?" is a favorite, followed by "Who are your favorite authors?" The old man sitting by the door surprised me when he raised his hand.

"Wendell Berry. His fiction is good, but his essays are better. And I love his poetry."

"Give us a poem, Odell," one of the women said.

The man stood and looked at the floor for a minute, and then raised his head and stared out a nearby window and spoke slowly and with deliberation:

> Sit and be still
> until in the time
> of no rain you hear
> beneath the dry wind's
> commotion in the trees
> the sound of flowing
> water among the rocks,
> a stream unheard before,
> and you are where
> breathing is prayer.

You could have knocked me over with a feather, but the women in the group just smiled and nodded as if this was an everyday experience. I remained speechless for a minute. When I finally found my voice, I asked, "What is your name, sir?"

"I'm Odell McPherson, ma'am. Nice to meet you."

"It's wonderful to meet you too, Mr. McPherson. Thanks for sharing those lovely words with us today."

As we milled around visiting after the meeting ended, I noticed that Miss Eleanor was putting leftover sandwiches and chips into a grocery sack, which she handed to Mr. McPherson as he left. I approached her as she cleaned up in the little kitchenette where she had prepared lunch.

"So, what's his story—Mr. McPherson?"

"Oh, he's a jewel, isn't he? Been coming to our meetings for a couple of years now, and checks out more books from the library than any other patron in town."

"Yes, I can tell he is well read, but—I don't know how to ask this delicately—does he have anyone to help him, like with his laundry and bathing and such?"

The woman laughed. "I can see how you would wonder about that. Truth is Odell has been homeless for some time now. Sleeps here and there. Takes a shower from time to time at a truck stop. He likes to joke about being the only person in town with a library card with no address on it. He knows we trust him to return the books he checks out, because he's always wanting some more."

"I don't get it. How can someone so intelligent end up homeless?"

She smiled. "It's a long story. But the short version is that Odell likes his liquor. His wife was the love of his life, and when she died he kind of went crazy. Let their home get so run down the county condemned it as a fire hazard. He eventually lost it, and didn't seem to care. Likes being in nature."

"You know, the main library in Memphis recently opened its doors for homeless people to sleep there on cold nights. Isn't there a shelter or something available here in Eupora? And where does he get money for food—and alcohol?"

"Social security checks. He has a post office box where he picks them up every month. And no, there aren't any shelters here."

"Wow. I wish I could do something to help him."

"Get in line. Everyone in town has tried one thing or another, but he doesn't seem interested in finding a place to live or changing anything else about his situation. Well, thanks so much for driving down to speak with us today. You heading back to Memphis now?"

"Thanks for inviting me. And yes, I'll be on my way."

As I walked to my car, I noticed an old Victorian house across the street from the library. Its yard was overgrown, but it had obviously been a place of beauty at one time. Potted plants crowded the front porch, which had a broken swing on one end. A graying picket fence surrounded the yard, its white paint nearly peeled off. Just as I was about to get into my car, I saw an elderly woman open the front door and step onto the porch holding a watering can. Her gray hair was in a loose bun, and her eyes twinkled as she smiled and waved. I returned the wave, and then walked up the sidewalk to her front porch.

"Good afternoon," I offered as I approached.

"Well, hello there. What brings you to my porch today?"

"I'm Adele Covington. I just spoke at the Friends of the Library's meeting, and I saw you on your porch and wanted to introduce myself."

"Well, come on inside." She set down her watering can and opened the door to her house. "All my porch chairs are broken, and it's still a bit chilly for my old bones, or we could sit outside."

"Thank you, Mrs.—?"

"I'm Francine Pittman. *Miss* Pittman, actually, but please call me Francine. I don't have much company these days. Would you like some iced tea?"

"That would be lovely."

I followed Francine where she indicated the chairs at the kitchen table. "Can I help you with the tea, Miss Pittman?"

She turned from the counter where she was getting two glasses from a cabinet and smiled.

"It's Francine, remember? And no, thank you." She brought over a glass pitcher of tea, followed by two glasses of ice and a small bowl of lemon slices. A sugar bowl and a plate of shortbread cookies were already on the table. "I love your hair, by the way. Those blond highlights really set off your blue eyes. Reminds me of myself when I was young and wore my hair short, in a bob like yours."

"Well, thank you. I bet you were stunning—you still are! And it sure looks like you are accustomed to entertaining guests, Francine." I sipped the icy tea and nibbled a cookie. "*Mmm*, these are amazing!"

"I don't cook much anymore, but shortbread has always been my specialty." She joined me at the table. "So, how does a busy author have time for an old lady like me?"

"Well, I grew up in Jackson and went to school up the road in Oxford, but never visited Eupora until today. I'm actually curious about the town and its residents. Especially Odell McPherson. Do you know him?"

Francine laughed. "Of course. Everyone knows Odell. Did he come to the meeting today and scandalize you by his attire?"

Busted! I blushed slightly and nodded.

"And I bet he quoted poetry or waxed eloquent on some literary topic."

"Exactly. I was so taken with him, but I'm also worried about his living situation. As I looked over at your house when I was leaving the library, I had an idea. Now, you might think I'm poking my nose in other people's business—and I guess I am—but I was thinking how you could use some help keeping up this beautiful home, and Odell could use a roof over his head."

I immediately regretted my inappropriate invasion, but Francine surprised me with her reply.

"I've actually thought about that too, but I've never thought that

Odell would go for it. He won't take charity, and he's ashamed of his alcohol problem."

"But it wouldn't be charity if he was helping you with repairs and upkeep on your house, would it? Of course, I can understand if you wouldn't want someone here who had a drinking problem."

I finished my tea and Francine reached for the pitcher to refill my glass.

"Oh, that wouldn't be a problem. I was an alcoholic for many years myself, so I understand addiction. But I got sober when I was in my sixties."

"So, maybe you could even help Odell."

"People only stop drinking when they want to, Adele."

"What led you to drink too much, and how did you quit, if you don't mind my asking."

"Not at all. I went to school with Eudora Welty, and she inspired me to write. But I was so nervous about getting my work out into the world that I started drinking every night. I was in my thirties then. What started as a nip or two of brandy turned into several glasses of wine, and eventually several glasses of bourbon. This went on for about twenty-five years. My drinking cost me my marriage, and I never had children, so I was alone and depressed. Needless to say, I never got my novel published. By the time I got sober, I was ready to work on my health, which is pretty much all I've done for the past twenty years."

"So, I know it's rude to ask, but how old are you?"

Francine laughed. "I just turned eighty. Been living in this house my whole life."

"And what is your book about?"

"Oh, it's a Southern gothic story. I always loved Faulkner's *Sanctuary*, so I tried to spin a dark tale about a small-town socialite who disappeared on the night of the debutante ball. I called it *Coming Out*."

"And you haven't tried to get it published? You could still do that!"

"Oh, goodness, no. I'm too old to deal with all of that now." She rose and walked to the counter, leaning on one arm and holding her back with the other. "Excuse me while I stretch for a minute. If I sit too long, I get stiff and my arthritis acts up."

"Of course. But don't change the subject on me. I have a neighbor in Memphis who is in her eighties, and she has published three books and is writing another. You can do this if you want to."

"You are so sweet, but it's all I can do to get out of bed, get dressed, and fix some food each day. By the time I do a little cleaning and small repairs around the house, I don't have any energy left. I missed my window to be an author, and that's just fine."

"But don't you see?" I walked to the kitchen counter and stood face-to-face with Francine. "If Odell was here to help you with the house, you could get that book published. Won't you at least think about it?"

Francine patted my arm and smiled. "Your enthusiasm is heartwarming, Adele. Thanks for the visit. It's time for my afternoon nap, so I'll see you to the door."

On my drive home to Memphis, all I could think about was Odell sleeping in some lean-to in the woods or at best an abandoned building downtown. I pictured him reading Robert Penn Warren by candlelight, huddled up under a pile of cardboard and dirty newspapers. And then my mind would jump back to Francine, alone in her century-old home with a potential best-selling manuscript stuffed away in a box in the attic. How could I get in touch with Odell and tell him about my idea?

The next day I called Miss Eleanor at the Eupora library and told her about my visit with Francine and my scheme for getting Odell to board with her in exchange for doing upkeep on the house.

"What did Francine say?" Miss Eleanor asked.

"Just what you'd imagine. That she figured Odell was too proud to accept the offer—that he might see it as charity. But we won't know that unless we try."

I'm sure Miss Eleanor could hear the passion in my voice.

"Okay. All I can do is mention it to him the next time he comes in to exchange books. It will be up to him to talk with Francine about it. You are so sweet to be concerned, but don't hold your breath. Oh, and I hope you'll come back and speak to our group again. Let us know when you've got another book coming out."

Sure enough, Odell McPherson showed up at the library about a week later, turning in several books and checking out new ones. "Got anything by Curtis Wilkie?" he asked Miss Eleanor, wiping his runny nose on the back of his filthy jacket.

"We've got *The Fall of the House of Zeus*. Read that one yet?"

"Nope. Sounds good. Anything new on the shelves?"

"Just got Michael Farris Smith's latest, *The Fighter*. Want to take a look?"

"What do you know about it?"

"He's being compared to Larry Brown and William Gay. Dark and gritty but also some fine literary prose. Just up your alley, I'd think."

"Okay, I'll take 'em both."

"By the way, I got a call from that author lady who was here last week, Adele Covington."

"Yeah? What did she want?" Odell put both the books into a backpack that was stuffed with bottled water, several packages of Nabs, and a few pieces of fruit.

"You might want to sit down for this, Odell. Seems she's taken an interest in your welfare."

"*Hrmph*. Her and everyone else, but she doesn't even know me. What's the deal?"

"Well, when she was leaving here last week, she saw Francine

Pittman out on her porch, and ended up with an invitation inside for a visit. Sounds like they had a long talk about Francine's situation—and yours."

"Like that's any of her business—big city gal coming down here trying to change my life. She's probably had it up to here with all the people living on the streets in Memphis and just sees me as another *case* she can fix or something."

"I don't think it's like that, Odell. She actually had a good idea, and Miss Pittman didn't seem too opposed. You might want to walk across the street and ask her about it. Couldn't hurt."

Odell shook his head, thanked Miss Eleanor for the books, and headed out the door. Just as he was about to walk off in the opposite direction of Francine's house, he heard her calling him.

"Odell! Odell McPherson! I know you see me out here on my porch. Come on over for a spell. I've got something to talk to you about."

He stopped walking for a minute, but then took back off on his way until she added, "And I've got a pot roast and mashed potatoes just about done—way more food than I can eat."

That did it. He turned and headed back towards her house. As he walked through the gate, he noticed how much work the fence needed. And her shrubs and flower beds were an overgrown mess. *Shame to let such a beautiful place go down like this.*

Inside, things weren't in much better shape. Wallpaper was peeling in lots of places, knobs were missing off cabinet doors in the kitchen, and the leak in the faucet was enough to drive a person crazy, if they could hear it.

"Can I use your bathroom to wash up?"

"Sure, it's just down the hall."

Francine set two places at the kitchen table and served their plates from the stove. When Odell returned to the kitchen, she spoke to him as though his being there for lunch were an everyday occurrence.

"Could you get the cornbread from the oven?" she asked, as she opened the refrigerator to retrieve the butter.

Odell hadn't eaten a meal on fine china in many years. Francine's Homer Laughlin Eggshell might have been chipped in a few places, but it still held its patina and charm. The aroma of the roast beef, which melted in his mouth, almost sent him crooning. He poured gravy on his mashed potatoes, slathered his cornbread with butter, and closed his eyes to enhance the pleasure.

"The Hankins boy was supposed to bring me some butter peas from the farmer's market, but he said they weren't in yet, so we'll have to settle for green beans."

"Does he do all your shopping for you?" Odell asked.

"Him and sometimes the Carter sisters, since they live nearby."

"So, Miss Eleanor tells me that Memphis author lady came to see you the other day. What was that about?"

"She was just being nice is all. Had an idea I think we should consider."

She went on to tell him about my suggestion that Odell take over maintenance and upkeep of her house and yard in exchange for room and board.

"What would people think, me living here with you and all?" Odell asked in between bites of cornbread.

"Well, they'd think it's a good thing you're not sleeping out there on the street or in the woods without decent food. And they'd be glad I had someone to keep this old house from falling on me in my sleep."

They both laughed.

"What about my drinking?" Odell put his fork down and stared at his lap, where he had dropped his hands. "I can't guarantee that I'll stop."

"Odell, there are no rules in this house, 'cept to be kind. I understand about the liquor—it had me in its grips for many years before I quit it a while back. And maybe you'll find that you don't need it as much if you've got a warm place to sleep, something to do with your hands, good food on the table, and someone to talk to."

"When you say it like that, how can I refuse? But I'm going to earn my keep. Starting with fixing that porch swing so we can sit out there and listen to the birds."

Several months went by before I heard from Francine. She got my phone number from Miss Eleanor at the library.

"Francine? Is that you? It's so nice to hear from you. How are you?"

"I'm just fine, thank you. But I could use your help."

"Of course. Have you finally decided to talk with Odell about my idea? Do you need me to help you convince him?"

She laughed heartily into the receiver. I heard something in the background that sounded like a lawn mower.

"Don't need your help with that. Odell moved in a couple of months ago. He's outside mowing the grass right now, and he's already fixed the gate and painted the fence and lots of other things. And here's the most surprising thing of all—he quit drinking. Decided he didn't need it anymore since he has a purpose now, and someone to share life with."

Tears welled as I listened to the happy lilt in her voice.

"That's all so amazing. I couldn't be happier. So, what is it you need my help with?"

"Well, you'll never believe it, but Odell found the manuscript for my novel in the attic, read it, and is pushing me to get it published."

"Oh, that's wonderful!"

"Problem is, I don't have a clue how to go about doing that. I know I need an editor, maybe an agent, in order to get a publisher, right?"

"There are several ways to go about this. I know some good freelance editors, so that would be a good place to start. They aren't cheap, but you need to get the manuscript polished before shopping it out. Do you have it on a computer or just a hard copy?"

"Believe it or not, I've got both. I saved it on a floppy disk back in the day, and of course I printed it out. Where do I start?"

"You can get a floppy disk converter from Amazon so you can save it to a flash drive. That way you can send it to an editor. Do you use email on your computer?"

"Yep. Sure do."

"Perfect. I'll send you a link to the converter on Amazon. When you get it, call me and I'll talk you through the process. Then we'll send it off to a freelance editor to get the ball rolling. I can't believe you're doing this! Meanwhile, please tell Odell hello for me. I'm so happy for you both!"

A few days later Francine called and I talked her through converting the manuscript into a Word document. Then I gave her the email address of an editor I knew, and she sent it off. Over the next few weeks they worked together to polish the book, and she was ready to find a publisher.

"I'm too old to go through an agent query—and I don't want to wait that long. Let's just send it to some small presses. Can you recommend a few?"

I looked through an online database and found several that accepted Southern literary fiction—one even specified gothic—and sent their links to Francine. She decided to send personalized query letters to all three. Two of them asked to see the full manuscript, so she sent it to them electronically. A few weeks later she received a rejection email from one.

Francine had just about put the novel out of her mind when her phone rang. Odell answered.

"Hello. Yes, who's calling? Just a minute please. Francine! Telephone." Francine was out on the porch, repotting a gardenia plant that had outgrown its container thanks to Odell's care.

"I'm busy. It's probably another one of those people trying to sell me something. If not, just take a message."

Odell walked out onto the porch. "It's someone who wants to talk about your manuscript. I think you should come talk to her!"

Francine wiped the dirt from her hands on her apron and hurried inside to the kitchen—as much as an eighty-something woman can hurry. Odell had left the receiver on the kitchen counter.

"Hello. Yes, this is Francine Pittman. Miss who? Can you speak up please? I'm a little hard of hearing. Oh, yes, Miss Barksdale from Kudzu Press. Nice to hear from you." Francine smiled at Odell. "Yes? Really? That's wonderful!" She gave Odell a thumbs up. "What do I need to do next? Sure. What's the editor's name? Okay I'll watch for the email. Thank you so much!"

She almost dropped the receiver trying to hang it up. She found Odell's arms and fell into them in an embrace. Odell eased her to the kitchen table and poured two glasses of lemonade.

"I can't believe it. They want to publish my book!" They toasted, clicking their lemonade glasses.

"That is wonderful news. But I'm not at all surprised. I told you that was a good book you wrote. What else did they say?"

"They want me to look at some notes from one of their editors— to make a few revisions. I should get those from them in a few days. Oh, let's call Adele and tell her!"

About a year later, I found myself driving back down Interstate 55, but this time I didn't go all the way to Eupora. I turned off at Highway 7 and drove into Oxford, winding my way through town and parking on the square. It was almost five, and Francine's reading at Off Square Books was in a half hour.

When I walked into the bookstore, the staff was just finishing setting up chairs for the event and putting out sparkling cider and cheese and crackers. Francine was up front near the podium, but I didn't see Odell. Then I heard his voice, but I couldn't believe it was him—clean hair, a trimmed beard, and a fresh pair of khaki pants and a button-down collar shirt.

"Wow. You clean up good." We hugged, and I was happy to smell aftershave instead of body odor and liquor on his breath.

"Yeah. I guess a good woman can do that for a man. Or in my case, two good women. No telling where I'd be right now if you hadn't come along. And I'm so danged proud of her—with her book getting published and all that. I think old man Faulkner would be proud, too."

"Me too."

I bought a copy of Francine's book and approached the stage where she was preparing for her reading. She reached out her arms, her face glowing with joy. We held each other for a minute, and then I put my copy of her book on the table in front of her. "Would you please inscribe my book for me?"

She took her pen, opened the book, and wrote, *For Adele, without whom I would never have believed I could do this. Francine Pittman.*

As the crowd gathered, I sat in the front row next to Odell, clutching my copy of the book to my heart, fighting back tears as one of the booksellers stood at the podium to introduce Francine. I thought my heart would burst as I heard her say, "Please welcome Miss Francine Pittman, author of an exciting new Southern gothic novel, *Coming Out.*"

ABERDEEN

Charlotte

A s I drove into Aberdeen to speak to the Friends group, I turned down Commerce Street to see the Magnolias—Aberdeen's jewel of antebellum architecture. The home is open to the public for tours and is also a destination for weddings, receptions, and other special events. Its magnificent magnolia trees were no longer in bloom on this day in early October, but I could imagine their beauty in the summer. I hoped I would have time for a tour after speaking at the library. The Evans Memorial Library prides itself on a wealth of genealogical material, historical research data, and its monthly Friends of the Library Lunch. Miss Hazel Crenshaw, president of the Friends group, greeted me.

"We're so excited to have you, Adele. To drive all the way down from Memphis to speak to our little group, well, it's an honor."

"The honor is all mine, Miss Hazel. Your library has quite a reputation for drawing some best-selling authors to your little town. And now I understand why they come."

"What do you mean?" Miss Crenshaw asked as she led the way from the library entrance to the meeting room in the back.

"Well, Aberdeen itself. It's so pretty, and historic. I drove past the Magnolias coming in. I'd love to take a tour."

"Well, you're in luck, because one of the guides there is a young woman who is a member of our Friends group, Charlotte Graham. She should be here today, and I think the house is open for tours this afternoon."

As we settled into the meeting room, Miss Hazel introduced me to some of the other members who had already arrived, including Miss Betty and her sister Miss Brenda, who were serving up plates of chicken salad and fruit Jell-O.

"Can I get you a co-cola or some lemonade?" Miss Betty asked.

"I'd love a Coke, thank you."

More members drifted in until the crowd reached around twenty, including Charlotte.

"Oh, Charlotte," Miss Hazel called as Charlotte found a seat at one of the long tables in the room, which had been decorated with autumn leaves and pumpkins and even a few cut-outs of ghosts and goblins. "Our speaker today would like to meet you."

Charlotte looked to be in her mid to late twenties, slim and attractive, with long, sandy blond hair. Her right arm was in a cast below the elbow. She looked up from her luncheon plate as I approached.

"Oh, me? Why? . . . I mean, it's so nice to meet you, Mrs. Covington."

"Oh, please call me Adele. What on earth happened to your arm?"

She blushed. "Oh, that. I was changing a light bulb in the ceiling at the house and fell off the ladder. I've always been clumsy that way."

"Oh, dear. Well I hope it heals soon. Miss Hazel tells me you give tours over at the Magnolias. I would love to see it. Are you available this afternoon?"

Charlotte's face lit up. "I'd love to. We don't have any groups scheduled this week—lots of weeks are like that in a small town—but I can give you a private tour."

"That would be wonderful. I read about the house online before I drove into town today. Can't wait to see it in person."

Miss Hazel waited patiently during our exchange. "It's time for our meeting to start. If you'll just have a seat up by the podium, I'll give a short introduction."

As Miss Hazel told the group about my growing up in Mississippi, going to school at Ole Miss, which was only about eighty miles from Aberdeen, and about the books I had written, I watched Charlotte cringe as she picked up a glass of lemonade with her right hand and quickly set it back down. I hoped that taking me to tour the Magnolias wouldn't cause her any more pain. My thoughts were interrupted as Miss Hazel finished her introduction, and I stood up at the podium.

"What a great Friends group y'all have here!" I opened my remarks and looked around the room at the fifteen to twenty people—mostly older, as usual—who were enjoying their lunches and one another's company. "I usually ask folks at these library groups how many of them are school teachers or retired school teachers, but today I'd like to know if any of y'all are artists, or have a special interest in art."

Three people raised their hands, including Charlotte.

"Wonderful! What kind of art do you do?"

One older woman mentioned oil portraits, and another said she was taking watercolor lessons at the community center. "Sometimes we paint outside. We're studying landscapes."

Charlotte sat quietly, so I addressed her directly. "What about you, Charlotte? You raised your hand."

She blushed. "Yes. I've done some abstracts, mostly with acrylics."

"Ah!" I smiled. "Have you read my novel yet?"

She nodded and returned a smile.

"Well, maybe I'll read a section about Elaine deKooning, the famous abstract expressionist painter."

"Yes, and please read a scene from the classroom at SCAD!" Charlotte said.

"Okay, I can do that. For anyone who doesn't know—or hasn't read the book yet—SCAD is Savannah College of Art and Design, which is in Savannah, Georgia. Although the book is fiction, most of it is set in real places, and of course deKooning was a real person. But the protagonist, a young girl named Mare, is completely fictional."

I read a few excerpts and then asked if there were any questions. One woman wanted to know whether the book was autobiographical—a common question at these events—and I answered that yes, I shared some of Mare's experiences, including sexual abuse and studying art.

"You should go to the Gumtree Museum of Art over in Tupelo," Miss Hazel said. "Some of Charlotte's paintings are there."

"Oh, I'd love to do that sometime—thanks for telling me." I noticed that Charlotte was looking down at the table, where her left hand sat gently on top of her right hand. I wondered how she could paint with her injury. I would ask later.

After the meeting, I asked Charlotte if we could go and see the Magnolias.

"Are you okay to drive, with your arm in the cast?"

"Oh, sure, I do it every day. It's not a big deal. You said you drove past the Magnolias on your way here, so you know where it is. I'll just meet you there in a few minutes."

I took a circuitous route from the library to the Magnolias in order to enjoy more of Aberdeen's charm. Formed in 1849, it has examples of almost every period and style of Southern architecture: antebellum cottages and mansions, ornate Victorians, turn-of-the-century neoclassical homes, and also bungalows from the 1920s and 1930s. Just under 5,500 people dwell on the town's eleven square miles of land, but they seem to have worked hard to maintain its culture and beauty.

As I walked up the sidewalk to the entrance to the Magnolias, I found myself wishing it were spring so that I could see it with the azaleas and magnolias in bloom. I was swept away by its magnificent columned portico. I pictured its residents enjoying mint juleps while sitting in the white rocking chairs and watching the horse-drawn carriages going down Commerce Street. More historic treats, and Charlotte, awaited me inside.

Stepping through the elegant double doors—with their transoms and side lights—into the house was like stepping back in time. The first thing I saw was an exquisite mahogany double staircase with a Waterford chandelier suspended above the stair landing. Period furnishings were everywhere. It was a feast for the eyes.

"It takes your breath away, doesn't it?" Charlotte asked as she greeted me.

"Yes. Tell me more about this place."

"It was built in 1850 by a prominent planter and physician, Dr. William Alfred Sykes, and his wife. The Magnolias is an excellent example of late antebellum classic Greek revival architecture." Charlotte spoke without notes.

"Is it still in their family?" I asked.

"No. Five generations of the Sykes family lived here, and then it was purchased by Clarence Day in 1984. He donated the Magnolias to the City of Aberdeen in 1986 in memory of his parents, Christine and Clarence Day."

"How long have you been a tour guide here?"

"Oh, about a year. Tommy—he's my husband—works construction during the week and teaches martial arts at the community center on the weekends. I work several part-time jobs. We're saving up to have a baby."

"What else do you do?" I asked as we walked through the rooms, pausing for Charlotte to explain about various pieces of antique furniture, or the identity of the people in the photographs in some of the rooms.

"Well, I teach art down at Hamilton Attendance Center two days a week, and I give tours here when people sign up for them. And sometimes one of my paintings actually sells." She laughed. "Abstract art isn't extremely popular around here. Folks just don't understand it. But it's one of the things I loved about your book."

"Thank you, Charlotte. I had fun researching that part of the book, since I never studied abstract expressionism in school. But I've always been a fan of it. Where did you study art?"

"I majored in art at 'the W'—Mississippi University for Women. Gosh, I could talk to you all day. Would you like to sit out back for a bit?"

"Sure."

She led me through the back door and onto a patio. "The arbor is beautiful in the spring when it's covered with roses."

We sat on one of the benches that looked out into the yard. A breeze lifted her hair away from her forehead and I noticed what looked like an old bruise beside her right eye. "Oh, dear. Did you hurt your face when you fell from the ladder?" I asked.

"What? Oh—that." She brushed her hair back in place with her hand and looked at her lap, placing her left hand on top of her right one, as if she was trying to hide her cast. "Yeah, I guess so."

We sat quietly for a moment, and then I said, "Charlotte, what's really going on?"

Her eyes filled with tears. "I can't really talk about it. I mean, Tommy would be so mad if I told anyone. He's not a bad person. But sometimes he just gets frustrated with me. I'm not a very good cook or housekeeper. When he comes home from a hard day of work, he expects certain things. But I get busy working on a painting in my studio and forget about the time and his supper isn't ready."

"And so, what, he hits you?"

She looked away.

"You know you can tell me, since I don't know Tommy or much of anyone else here in Aberdeen. I'm a safe place for you to land with this."

I reached over to put my hand on her shoulder, and she fell into my arms, sobbing heavily. I held her for a few minutes and then she sat back up. I found a Kleenex in my purse and offered it to her.

"How often does this happen?"

"Not often, really. Maybe once a month or so. We've been married for two years, and it's gotten worse recently."

"You need to call the police, Charlotte. And I know this isn't what you want to hear, but you need to get away from him. If his anger is escalating, you could end up dead."

"I don't have anywhere to go. My parents are both dead, and I don't have any brothers or sisters. Tommy was my high school sweetheart. He went to work straight out of twelfth grade, and we got married the week after I graduated from the W. We're renting a little house on the edge of town."

I thought about Miss Hazel and the other sweet people I had met at the library. A small Southern town like Aberdeen was sure to have someone who could take Charlotte in, just long enough for her to figure out what to do about Tommy.

"We need to get you somewhere safe," I said. "And then you need to call the authorities and get a restraining order against Tommy. Isn't there anyone we can call?"

"Well, there is this one teacher at the Attendance Center. She lives by herself, about fifteen minutes from here."

"Let's call her. Now."

I waited outside while Charlotte went back into the house and called her friend on her cell phone. As she walked back onto the patio, I heard her say, "Thank you so much, Barbara. I'll be there in about an hour."

"Sounds like that was a *yes*," I said.

Charlotte nodded. She stared out into the yard with a faraway look. She moved slowly towards the bench where we had been sitting, as if waiting for someone to tell her what to do next.

"Do you need help packing up some of your things?"

"What?" She turned her head towards me quickly as if she had forgotten I was there. "Oh, no, thank you. You need to get on the road back to Memphis if you're going to make it before dark. I'll be fine. I'm just going to grab a few things and head over to my friend's place."

"Okay. Here's my cell phone. Call me if you need anything." I handed her a business card, and we embraced.

Barbara Mosely had been teaching English for twenty-five years. She was about the same age as Charlotte's mother, were she still alive—a quintessential old maid schoolteacher. Charlotte arrived at the door of her two-bedroom farmhouse with a suitcase in her left hand and a backpack over her shoulder.

"Oh, sweetie, I'm so glad you called. I've been worried about you, but I didn't think it was any of my business." She took Charlotte's suitcase and led her into the kitchen, where a teakettle whistled and a sweet aroma wafted from the oven.

"Would you like a cup of tea and a fresh scone?"

"Oh, wow. That would be lovely, thank you." Charlotte's eyes were red and puffy, and her hand shook as she took the teacup from Barbara.

"I can't believe I'm here—that I'm actually doing this." She looked at Barbara's face. "Oh, I'm so ashamed."

"You have nothing to be ashamed of. It's Tommy that should be ashamed. And we're going to make sure he never hurts you again. I've alerted the sheriff that you're here. Tommy doesn't know where you are, does he?"

"Maybe not yet, but when he gets home from work and reads my note he's going to be furious."

"What did you say in the note?"

"That I was leaving. That he wasn't going to hurt me anymore."

"You know," Barbara said as she poured them both more tea, "it's

Tommy who should be moving out of the house—not you. But one step at a time. The main thing is that you are safe now. I've made up the bed in the guest room with fresh linens and there are clean towels in the bath. I want you to make yourself at home."

"Okay, but I'm supposed to teach tomorrow. What if Tommy comes to the school looking for me?"

"Sheriff Johnson is going to have one of his deputies at the school. Now you just take a warm bath and get some sleep."

That night, Charlotte stirred restlessly, waking in a sweat once and thinking she heard noises outside the house several times. About three in the morning she heard a loud crash from the front of the house. Grabbing her cell, she hurried to the window and looked through the curtains. Tommy's truck was outside. She dialed 911 just as he burst into the room after kicking in the front door. She dropped her phone behind her back, leaving it on so the operator could hear her and track the call.

"Tommy! What are you doing here?" She spoke loudly. Tommy caught on.

"Give me that fuckin' phone!" He shoved her and smashed the phone under his foot. Grabbing her good arm, he pulled her away from the bed, but Barbara appeared in the doorway.

"Leave her be!" Barbara shouted with all the authority of a seasoned schoolteacher, both arms behind her back.

"Yeah? Or what?" Tommy yelled.

"The police will be here any minute, Tommy," Charlotte said.

As he turned to Charlotte, Barbara smashed a vase over his head, knocking him to the floor. "Quick! Get out of here!"

Barbara pulled Charlotte out of the room and outside to her car. As she put the car in reverse, Tommy appeared at the front door. They hurried out the driveway and down the street, passing a squad car with blue lights flashing heading the opposite way. They pulled into a neighbor's driveway and turned around.

"Do you think it's safe to go back now?" Charlotte asked.

"Let's give them a few more minutes. Are you okay? Did he hurt you?"

"No, I'm fine, thanks to you."

Tommy was handcuffed and jailed, and Charlotte returned to her home the next day. The sheriff assured her that Tommy wasn't getting out any time soon. She was safe, and he encouraged her to hire a lawyer. With Barbara as a witness to the break-in, and Charlotte's bruises and broken arm as evidence of his recent assaults, Tommy didn't have a chance. He would be in jail for a long time.

Charlotte called Tommy's brother, who worked with him in construction, to come and get Tommy's things from the house. The next week she filed for a divorce. There wouldn't be any alimony since Tommy was in jail and couldn't work.

Charlotte began to worry about making rent on the house and other bills. Her part-time teaching job and the little bit she made giving tours at the Magnolias weren't nearly enough. She would be without medical insurance, since she would no longer be covered by Tommy's job.

A couple of months later she returned to the library for its December Friends meeting. The library and the meeting room were decorated with greenery and little white lights everywhere. Elves on shelves appeared to be reading books. Hot chocolate and eggnog were ready to serve at the meeting. The group didn't have a visiting author for their Christmas event, which was really more of a party. Everyone greeted Charlotte with hugs and encouragement.

"We're sorry about what you've been through," Miss Hazel said, "but we're so glad that Tommy is out of your life. We've all been worried about you."

"I guess there aren't any secrets in a small town, are there?" Charlotte asked.

"No," said Miss Hazel, "and no one is ever really alone here, either."

Barbara Mosely walked in. She wasn't a member of the Friends group and usually taught on weekdays, when their meetings were held, but the kids were out for Christmas holidays.

"What are you doing here?" Charlotte asked.

"Well, that's a fine howdy do," Barbara smiled and gave Charlotte a hug. After their embrace she looked her up and down and added, "So glad to see you got that cast off. It'll be a lot easier to paint now."

Charlotte shrugged. She hadn't painted since Tommy broke her arm. "So, are you going to join the Friends group? What about teaching?"

"No, I'm just here as a visitor for the Christmas party. And I have some official news from the school that I wanted to share with you when you were among your friends here at the library."

"And also me!" I had been waiting for my cue, and slipped through the crowd with an armful of balloons. "Congratulations!"

"Adele? Wait—congratulations for what? That's not usually something people say when someone gets a divorce." Charlotte looked confused.

I smiled at Miss Hazel and looked at Barbara. "I think you'd better tell her the news, Barbara."

All eyes were on Barbara as she stepped to the front of the crowd and looked at Charlotte.

"The Attendance Center has given me permission to extend you an offer of a full-time teaching position starting next semester. With full medical benefits!"

Everyone cheered and Charlotte was speechless. She hugged Barbara again, and then turned to me.

"I can never thank you enough for giving me the courage to stand up to Tommy. If you hadn't come to town back in October and we hadn't had that conversation at the Magnolias, no telling what my life might be like now."

"You were just ready to do what you needed to do is all," I said.

"And thankfully you've got all these great people in this community supporting you. Oh, and I've got one more surprise."

"More? What more can there be?" Charlotte said.

"A friend of mine in Memphis—an art collector—visited the Gumtree a few weeks ago and loved your paintings. She wants to commission you to do some for her. And she has mentioned you to the owner of a swanky gallery in East Memphis who might want to host a show for you."

Charlotte had been holding back tears, but the dam burst with that final bit of news. For the rest of the party everyone talked about which books they were going to read the following year, and which authors they planned to invite.

When it was time to leave, I said my goodbyes—promising to stay in touch, of course—and drove down Commerce Street to take a look at the Magnolias, which was decked out in its Christmas finery. And then I drove by Charlotte's house, glad to see that she hadn't gotten home from the library yet. I walked to the back of my car and pulled out a large package. I dropped it off on her porch quickly and hurried away in my car, heading home to Memphis.

A little while later Charlotte drove up and found the package leaning against her front door. She pulled it inside and carried it to her couch so that she could sit down to open it. Tearing off the butcher paper, she discovered several large, blank art canvases inside. A note was attached: *"They always say time changes things, but you actually have to change them yourself."—Andy Warhol*

OXFORD

Avery

Arriving at the Lafayette County and Oxford Public Library felt more like being back on sorority row at Ole Miss. My mind was immediately flooded with memories of my time as a student at this school that has always been known for having the most beautiful girls in the South—or anywhere. I changed clothes several times before driving down to Oxford, finally settling on a conservative black pencil skirt and pink sweater set. My mother's pearls and matching pearl earrings gave me what I hoped was a professional but not-too-stuffy look.

The library's redbrick exterior and tall white columns were adorned with a huge banner hanging from the second-floor balcony that read, *ARE YOU READY?* As I walked from the parking lot to the door—adding an intentional spring to my step and sway to my hips—I half expected a group of students to come pouring out of their cars yelling the iconic Ole Miss cheer, "HELL, YEAH! DAMN RIGHT! HOTTY TODDY . . ."

Named for the university town of Oxford, England, our Oxford is home to the state's first university, which opened its doors in 1848. But Ole Miss isn't Oxford's only attraction. In addition to good food, quaint boutiques, and one of the nation's most famous bookstores—Square Books, home to the Thacker Mountain Radio show—Oxford hosts year-round sporting, literary, and musical events.

Each March it hosts the Oxford Conference for the Book and the Double Decker Festival is in April. In June it provides the LOU Summer Sunset Series, the Oxford Film Festival, and the Yoknapatawpha Summer Writers' Workshop. The annual Faulkner and Yoknapatawpha Conference is in July.

It was into this magical cultural milieu that I went to speak at the library's "Books and Lunch" gathering, where brown bag lunches were offered free to anyone who signed up for the reading. A nice crowd showed up to hear me read from my novel. My protagonist is a runaway orphan who throws up graffiti and ends up with a scholarship to Savannah College of Art and Design (SCAD). So, I hoped to see lots of college kids at the reading. But as often happens at these library events, the audience was comprised mostly of teachers and retired teachers. As I was about to start, a tall, lanky young man walked in and sat in the back row of the small auditorium.

I had met Avery at the front desk of the library when I first arrived. He worked part time while writing for a local newspaper, and—here comes the best part—working on a fantasy novel.

After talking about my novel and reading a few selections, I opened the floor for questions. I could almost write the script for the Q&A time after doing so many of these readings.

"How did you become interested in graffiti?" "Have you ever actually seen a weeping icon?" "Why did you decide to write a book about three women who were all sexually abused?"

Avery's questions revealed his writer's heart. "How did you decide which point of view to use? Did you consider writing in first person? Was it difficult to mix real life persons and places with the fictional ones?"

I answered each of his questions with clipped answers, not wanting to bore the non-writers in the room but hoping later to speak privately with Avery.

"So, how old are you, Avery?" I asked after everyone else had left and he was helping me pack up the books that didn't sell at the event.

"I'm twenty-six. I know what you're thinking. Why is someone my age working part time in a library?" His self-effacing demeanor added to his charm. Six feet and change, with wavy brown hair tucked behind his ears, his long legs barely filled out his skinny jeans, which were topped off with a T-shirt that read, *Divergent.*

"Well, actually, I was wondering if you were a student."

"No. I did a couple of years at community college, but I couldn't seem to focus. I really just wanted to write."

"I hear you. So, tell me about your fantasy novel. What interested you about that genre?"

"It's a long story. I don't want to take up too much of your time. I'm sure you need to get on the road or something."

"Actually, I was going to stop at Square Books before leaving town. Can you get away and join me on their balcony for a cup of coffee?"

Avery looked at his phone and then glanced out the door of the auditorium into the library.

"Let me see how busy we are. Maybe I can take a break."

Driving around the square in Oxford was like flashing back in time. Like other small towns in the South, it was built around a central structure—a town hall that anchors its grid. Covered sidewalks line the stores fronting on the circle. Square Books still maintains a historic sign attached to its terra-cotta stucco exterior that reads, *Fortune's Famous Ice Cream.*

Inside the bookstore, shelves were filled with a multitude of works by famous and up-and-coming authors, many of whom lived, or had once lived, in Oxford and other Mississippi towns. It was at once inspiring and intimidating to be surrounded by such genius, and also thrilling to see my own novel on the shelves with some of those brilliant Mississippi authors.

I visited briefly with one of the employees, found my way upstairs, grabbed a latte from the coffee bar, and headed out to the balcony. My feet were killing me, so I took off the black leather heels I had chosen to wear, wishing I had opted for a comfy pair of sandals instead. In my mid-sixties, I still struggled to accept the limitations my aging body tried to put on my fashion sense.

Large green ferns hung in baskets above the balcony's railing. A breeze brought enticing smells from the nearby restaurant kitchens. The atmosphere was charged with memories of so many Saturday afternoons I had spent there in years past, when my writing group met monthly to critique each other's works in progress. It was still hard for me to believe that those chapters they helped me shape and the characters they helped bring to life on the pages of my novel were being read in this iconic bookstore. And now I was getting acquainted with a young writer starting on his own journey.

Avery found me outside a few minutes later and we sat in wicker chairs at one end of the balcony. He tossed his backpack on the table and looked at me expectantly. "Ms. Covington—you beat me here."

"Oh, please, Avery, call me Adele. It makes me feel much younger." I smiled as he blushed and ran his fingers through his hair. "And by the way, what's your last name?"

"Oh, that. It's Carmichael."

"So, you were going to tell me how you got interested in fantasy, Avery Carmichael." I smiled at his shyness and sipped my latte and watched as he seemed to consider his response.

"I started reading Robert Jordan's books when I was in high school. Especially the Conan the Barbarian series. But later I got into his Wheel of Time books. I loved being able to escape into a whole different world from the one I grew up in."

Avery's voice dropped off and he looked away.

"What was that world like?"

"Well, I was adopted when I was a baby. But my adoptive mom got pregnant right after they got me, so she had a biological son just a year younger than me."

"What was that like for you, growing up?"

"It was okay. I mean, they were nice to me and all that, but I never felt as close to my parents as my brother seemed to be. And I always felt like we were competing. But he was better at sports and was in the popular crowd and all that. I kind of gravitated towards the grunge kids. Got into drugs. My parents never had me tested, but I'm pretty sure I have ADD, so I was self-medicating with pot and other stuff." Avery paused long enough to light a cigarette and take a drink of his black coffee. "Do you mind if I smoke?"

"Not at all. That's what God made the fresh air for, right?" We both laughed, and I brought us back to the discussion at hand. "Tell me about your novel."

"It's kind of dystopian fantasy. Set in a future world where babies are warehoused away from their parents and then adopted out to couples they are matched with."

"Sounds like *The Handmaid's Tale.*"

"It's got some similarities, only it's not a Christian theonomy like the one that overthrew the government in that book. It's more like a neo-Nazi society, where the government is trying to put the best babies with the best parents to raise super beings."

"Avery, why on earth would you want to escape to such a world? I thought you were creating fantasy to find a better life than the one you had growing up."

"I know it sounds weird, but here's the thing. The protag is a kid who leads a group of rebels who want to find their birth parents."

I got it. Avery and I sat quietly for a few minutes. I looked at my watch and realized I needed to start driving home. I wanted to leave Avery with some encouragement.

"I think you've got a great idea there. Have you had anyone read what you've written so far?"

Avery shook his head.

"Look, I know it's scary showing your stuff to others for the first time, but if you ever want to publish a book, you've got to get some help. How much have you written so far?"

"About twenty-five thousand words."

"That's a great start! Hey—I know about a workshop you might want to look into. It's called the Yoknapatawpha Summer Writers' Workshop, and it's here in Oxford every May or June. I went to it seven years in a row, and it really helped. Want me to send you a link to the workshop's website? Actually, I can give you an email for the guy who organizes it."

"Sure, why not?"

Avery picked up his backpack and held the door for me as we left the balcony and headed back downstairs and out the front door of the bookstore. Laughter wafted down from the balcony bar at City Grocery, two doors down. Locals and students came and went from the shops and bars and restaurants all around the square. I loved the creative spirit that seemed to permeate this little patch of literary heaven.

"Thanks for taking time to visit with me, Adele," Avery said as I got my sunglasses out of my purse and put them on for the drive home.

"It was my pleasure. Good luck with your book." I gave Avery a quick hug goodbye and headed home.

Three months later Avery drove onto the Ole Miss campus and pulled up to the Depot—the 150-year old facility that was declared a Mississippi landmark in 1992. Back in the 1870s, the Depot bustled with students, faculty and visitors. Mail trains delivered packages and letters from family and friends. William Faulkner, who served as the college's postmaster at one time, gathered sacks of mail from the depot and carried them to the university's post office. After much renovation, the building became available for use by groups of up to sixty people in 2003. One of those groups was the Yoknapatawpha Summer Writers' Workshop.

Organized and led by faculty members in the MFA creative writing program at Ole Miss and other universities, the workshop was a weekend gathering of about fifteen mostly new and emerging writers who submitted samples of their works in progress to be critiqued by the faculty and their fellow participants. Everyone received copies of each other's writing ahead of time, and students were asked to be prepared to offer feedback during the workshop as well as pass along written notes on each manuscript. In addition to the critique sessions, authors, editors, literary agents, and publicists gave craft talks during the weekend. And of course there were social events like a night at Taylor Grocery for catfish, and a reading at Square Books, usually for one of the authors on faculty for the workshop.

Avery worried about others seeing—and worse yet, critiquing— his words. But that's what the shy boy had signed up for, and on Saturday morning the time came for his piece to be *workshopped,* as the process was called. First the workshop leader, an MFA grad named Grant, asked Avery to make a few introductory comments about his writing sample. Just as he started, a middle-aged woman walked in and quietly sat in a chair at the back of the room.

"Oh, wait just a minute, Avery. Let me introduce one of our speakers who has just arrived first. This is Julia Wilson, who teaches in the MFA program here at Ole Miss. Julia also has published several books of poetry, and she will be talking with us later this morning about how poetry affects prose in our first craft talk of the weekend. Welcome, Julia!"

Julia smiled and nodded. "Thanks, Grant. I didn't mean to interrupt. I promise to be quiet."

Grant laughed and indicated to Avery that he could give his introduction.

"It's a dystopian fantasy," Avery began. "The setting is somewhere in America in the future—maybe around the year 3,000. It's after a third world war, and the totalitarian government takes all newborn babies from their parents and puts them in warehouses until they are assigned to a new set of parents, with the most prominent members of society having first pick. Babies from lower-class birth parents are often left in the warehouses—which then become orphanages—and later trained to do mundane jobs. The protagonist, Balock, and his girlfriend, Ember, are leading a rebellion against the government, in order to stop this procedure and to find their birth parents. The manuscript I turned in is the opening chapter and—"

"Okay," Grant interrupted. He instructed Avery to stay quiet during his critique session, which would last about thirty minutes, and to take notes. Next, Grant gave a brief summary, commenting on how Avery was doing with world building and how the characters' stories connected emotionally with the reader. Then he opened up the floor to other participants.

Avery was asked about his choice to write in first-person present tense, and about his crafting of futuristic phrases, especially in the dialogue. Although Julia had promised to remain quiet, she piped up near the end of his session, complimenting his pacing and the lyrical quality of his writing.

"So, Avery, I was just wondering two things, actually. First of all, have you ever written poetry, or had any instruction in it? Your prose reflects a natural gift for rhythm. And the second question is why did you choose to write about a protagonist who was leading a crusade for himself and others to find their birth parents? There's such a strong emotional pull, even in this opening chapter."

Avery looked down at his laptop, on which he had taken notes during the critique session. He shifted nervously in his chair, clasped his hands together, and slowly looked up at Julia.

"Well, the first question is easy. I've always loved poetry—reading it and also writing a few mongrels myself, since I was a kid, really."

"Who did you read?" Julia asked.

"Mark Doty is a favorite. *Atlantis* was amazing. I also really like T. S. Eliot and Allen Ginsberg."

Julia nodded and waited for Avery to answer her second question.

"On the choice of my subject matter, that's really personal."

"Of course, you don't have to answer if you don't want to. But you should know that if you publish this book and give readings one day, people will probably ask you this same question. Readers often want to know what inspires authors' subjects. And if it's fiction, they want to know if any of the book is autobiographical."

Avery took a minute before answering. He looked at Grant, his eyes asking for a way out. Grant stepped in.

"She's got a point, Avery. But you seem uncomfortable with her question, so maybe you need to just sit with this for a while. Even reconsider if this is what you really want to write about. You could always—"

"Okay, so I was adopted. Is that what you wanted to know? Can't a person just write a book without everyone getting all up in his business?"

Avery slammed his laptop shut, tossed it into his backpack and left the room. He didn't want to miss Julia's craft talk, but he wasn't sure he could stand the way he was feeling one minute longer. Like someone was peeling off a layer of his skin.

He left the building and headed for his car, where he rolled down a window and lit a cigarette. He thought about dropping out of the workshop and just heading back to his apartment where he could hide out with his secrets. But everyone had been so encouraging about his book, about his writing. He had come here to learn how to be a writer, to make his book better, and he couldn't let his feelings interfere.

When he walked back into the Depot, everyone was milling around, getting another cup of coffee during the break. Julia was preparing for her presentation at the front of the room. Grant approached Avery and put his hand on his shoulder.

"Hey, man. I hope we didn't overstep back there. These workshops can get pretty intense. You okay?"

"Yeah, sure. I shouldn't have gone off like that. I guess I just wasn't prepared, emotionally, for how this would go."

"Just remember that it's your book. We're all just here to give you feedback. You decide what to do with it, kind of like what they say in twelve steps meetings: take what works and leave the rest."

Everyone found their seats and Grant stood to introduce Julia's craft talk. But first he made an announcement.

"Okay, everyone. It's time for our first craft talk of the weekend, but first I've got an announcement. One of our faculty members for the workshop just had a family emergency and had to cancel, so I invited Adele Covington, an author from Memphis, to come down and give a talk in his place tomorrow. In fact, Adele just texted me that she's almost here and will be joining us for this next session. Wait—here she is now."

I walked into the room and tried to duck quietly into a chair on the back wall, but Grant saw me and introduced me. Everyone turned around to the back of the room, and as I smiled and nodded, my eyes caught a familiar face—Avery! He smiled and gave a slight wave.

Julia handed out copies of excerpts from several works of prose. She asked the class to compare the pieces, looking for good use of rhythm and pacing in some, and economy of words in others. Next, she led them through a free-write session that involved childhood memories. Several people shared what they had written, and they discussed how to use those memories in their works in progress. Avery forgot about his earlier discomfort and lost himself in the session, enthused that he could apply the lessons to his own writing.

"It's time for lunch," Grant announced after the talk was over. "There are lots of places to eat on or nearby the square, so find someone you'd like to get to know better and head on out. Be back by one thirty for our next critique session."

After the talk, Avery found me in the back.

"Hey! I'm so glad you're here. Want to grab some lunch?"

"Sure, but Julia and I are old friends, so would it be okay if she joins us?"

Avery shrugged. "I guess so, sure."

Julia approached and we hugged.

"So, do you know Avery?" she asked.

"Yes, we met at an event at the library here a few months ago. We're about to go to lunch. Want to go with us?"

"I'd love to."

"I feel a bit out of my league here," Avery said. "A newbie fantasy writer, a novelist, and a published university poetry professor?"

"But then there's your love of poetry, right? That's unusual for someone writing in your genre."

"Guess it is. Sure, let's go have some lunch. Where would you like to eat?"

"The square is going to be crowded and most of the restaurants there are pretty noisy, so why don't we go somewhere a little less known to the tourists? How about the University Club?" Julia offered.

"Are you a member?" I asked.

"Yep. I use it to entertain visiting faculty sometimes. Let's take my car."

We parked behind the club and walked upstairs for lunch. As Julia had suggested, it wasn't crowded, and we found a table by a window.

"Welcome back, Miss Wilson," a waitress said, handing us each a menu and a glass of water. "What would y'all like for lunch?"

I ordered first: "The chicken salad plate sounds good," I said, "and sweet tea."

"Same for me," said Julia.

"I'll have the meatloaf, mashed potatoes, and green beans, please. Oh, and unsweetened tea," Avery said.

After we got our drinks, Julia sipped her tea and started the conversation. "So, Avery, your writing is lyrical, and you love poetry, but I think there's something more at work here than your writing.

How do you feel about telling us about your childhood?"

Avery and I exchanged looks, and then he repeated much of the same story he had told me on the balcony at Square Books earlier in the spring—about his adoptive family, his parents' birth son, and how he didn't fit in. He also talked about his ADD and subsequent drug use, and not finishing college.

"Full disclosure, Julia," I interrupted, "but Avery and I talked about some of this when I was here for the library event."

"Oh, I hope it doesn't feel like we're ganging up on you, Avery," said Julia.

"Well, I was a bit nervous coming to lunch with the two of you, but I really appreciate what you're trying to do. The workshop critique session was hard, emotionally, but I think it also cracked open my shell a bit."

"So, are you writing your fantasy novel as a way to create another universe, a different reality, than the one you grew up in?" Julia asked.

"I think so. I mean, a dystopian world can sound a little extreme, but you never know how quickly that other reality might become a present one."

Our food arrived and we ate quietly for a few minutes before Julia asked another question. "Have you ever wanted to search for your birth mother?"

Avery was caught a bit off guard but recovered himself as he swallowed another bite of meatloaf. "Yes, actually. But I haven't done anything about it yet. That's just like me, not to follow through with something, just like with my education."

"Why do you think you haven't searched for her yet?"

"Honestly, I think I'm afraid that if I found her, she wouldn't want me. It would be a worse rejection than the loneliness I feel with my adoptive family."

"But if you're not happy now, don't you think it would be worth the risk?" I asked.

"Maybe so." Looking at Julia he asked, "What about you? Do you have kids?"

"No. I actually never married."

"Wow. That's a surprise. I mean, you're attractive and smart and creative. Oh, I guess that sounds kind of demeaning, like you're not good enough if you're not a wife or mother. I didn't mean it like that. I was just—"

"It's okay." Julia reached across the table and touched Avery's hand. Their eyes met, and I felt a kindness pass between them. Julia continued, "I get that all the time, and I know you weren't being mean. I had some bad experiences with men, really with boys, when I was young, and I guess I just closed that door and poured myself into my career. I write my feelings into my poetry and pour my motherly instincts into my students."

"I can see that you're good at both of those things." Avery smiled and relaxed, maybe for the first time all day.

"Oops! Time to get you back to the workshop. I'll get the check."

"Oh, no, I can buy my own lunch."

"Not at the University Club, you can't. Only members."

Julia signed the check and we headed back to her car. The drive back to the Depot was mostly quiet, and when she pulled up into the parking lot, Avery said, "Aren't you two coming in?"

"No, my part is done. I was just here to give a craft talk," said Julia.

"And I've got some work to do on a manuscript, so I'm headed to my hotel room. But I'll see you tomorrow for my craft talk."

He wore his disappointment on his face. "Oh, okay. Well, thanks so much for the lunch, Julia. Hey, since I live in town, maybe we can have coffee sometime. And I was also wondering if maybe I could audit one of your poetry classes."

"Yes, to both of those! Now get back to the workshop and learn things!"

The afternoon critique sessions proved to be as emotion-packed as Avery's. Shannon, a girl who had been sexually molested by her grandfather, brought a chapter of her memoir in progress to the workshop. The other participants were kind in their criticisms of her writing, as was Grant, but the very act of sharing such personal events with a roomful of people had a similar effect on Shannon as Avery's simple confession that he was adopted.

An older man had turned in a chapter of his World War II novel, which focused on a veteran with post-traumatic stress disorder. The message was powerful, but the prose needed work, and the advice the writer received could mean the difference between another manuscript that got stuck in a drawer forever and a powerful novel that made its way onto the shelves of bookstores and libraries for future readers. Avery wasn't sure what he had expected from the workshop—sweet little stories about Southern romance and Great-Aunt Bess's apple pie?—but the emerging writers who brought their stories with them left with the tools they needed to turn their rough drafts into polished manuscripts.

When I walked into the Depot the next morning, I was glad to find Avery sharing some more relaxed chatter with his fellow students over coffee and doughnuts.

"Hi, Adele." We shared a hug, and he introduced me to one of his new friends. Grant opened the session with a few housekeeping notes, and it was my turn. My craft talk was on using scenes and active verbs to strengthen prose. The students did a few exercises and the hour was over quickly.

After another quick coffee break a panel formed in the front of the room. Everyone found their seats as the speakers from the weekend gathered for a final session, during which we would talk about the business end of writing—working with editors, literary agents, and publishers. One of the panel members was on faculty in the creative writing program at Ole Miss, like Julia was. One was a publicist. I took the third seat, and the fourth chair was empty. Five minutes after the panel was to begin, Grant addressed the room.

"Good morning. I hope everyone had fun at Taylor Grocery last night."

Smiles and murmurs filled the room.

"So, this morning we wanted to give y'all an opportunity to learn a bit about what to do with your manuscript once you've polished it, using some of the tools you gained during the workshop this weekend. I've invited the faculty who gave craft talks back to share their wisdom on this, and I apologize because Julia Wilson hasn't arrived yet. We'll go ahead and get started, and I'll try to reach her on her cell phone."

For the next hour, we talked about how to work with freelance editors to get the manuscript ready for its next step. We shared about the different paths to publishing, including the traditional paths of querying literary agents or independent presses, and the most recent trend of self-publishing.

I noticed Avery watch Grant leave the room during part of the session. We saw him through the window talking on his cell, and I wondered if something had happened to Julia. When the session was over and everyone was saying their goodbyes, we approached Grant.

"She's fine," Grant said. "Just something about a deadline she was chasing with her agent on her next book. It's really not like her to back out on a commitment, but I'm sure it was unavoidable."

Avery and I said goodbye to Grant and walked to my car.

"Are you going back to Memphis now?" he asked.

"Yeah, I need to get home."

He leaned against my car, hung his head, and moved the toe of his shoe across the gravel.

"Hey, are you okay? You opened up some old wounds in your conversation with Julia and me yesterday."

He nodded. "Yeah, I've definitely got a lot to think about. Thanks so much for spending time with me. Be safe driving home, and let's stay in touch."

We hugged and I took off.

Avery headed home, taking a different route to drive past Square Books and look up at the balcony where he and I had visited the day I spoke at the library. And then as he made his way around the roundabout and headed south down Lamar, he passed the University Club and thought about the things the three of us had talked about during our lunch. *Was that just yesterday?* He wished Julia had been on the panel at their morning session, and wondered if it would be weird of him to call her up just to talk sometime. He wasn't attracted to her romantically—and of course she was probably fifteen or twenty years older than him—but something about her drew him in.

Back to work at the library the next day, Avery thought about my visit in the spring, the day I talked at the Books and Lunch event. It was an easy reach to imagine himself doing that one day—speaking to a group of people about *his* book. But first he had to finish writing it. That was why he was only working part time, after all.

But the following days and weeks were difficult. He couldn't seem to keep his mind on the work. Every time he sat down to write— and immersed himself in the fantasy world he was creating on the page—his feelings about his birth mother grew stronger. The closer Balock and Ember got in their search for their birth parents in the book, the stronger his own desires grew. He remembered my words at lunch that day up at the University Club and wondered if I was right. Maybe it would be worth the risk.

Avery had been adopted through the Mississippi Children's Home in Jackson. He had looked them up online several years ago but never followed through. Their website didn't offer a link to search for birth parents, but it did have a phone number. His palms were sweaty as he punched the number into his cell.

"Mississippi Children's Home, this is Brenda."

"Um, yes, hello. My name is Avery Carmichael. I was adopted in 1992, and I was wondering how to initiate a search for my birth mother."

"Okay. I can help you with that, Mr. Carmichael. I assume you are calling because your adoptive parents used our placement services?"

"That's what they told me. So, is there some form I fill out, or what?"

"There are a couple of ways you can proceed. Of course, you are welcome to visit us in person if you'd like. Or there's an online form you can use."

"Are all the records open, or what?"

"No, actually some of the birth mothers haven't given their permission. But many have. How would you like to proceed?"

"Is there a fee?"

"Yes, one hundred twenty-five dollars, mostly to cover paperwork. You can pay by check or credit card, in person or online."

"How long does the search take?"

"Well, that depends. If your birth mother has also initiated a search, it could happen quickly. If not, you'll be looking at a longer search."

"Wow. This is surreal. I guess I'll do the online search. What's the link?"

The woman gave Avery the link to follow, and he filled out the form, including his credit card information, and was about to click SEND when a wave of nausea hit—the same old clouds of self-recrimination. *What if she doesn't want to meet me? What if we don't connect?* He took a deep breath and pushed the SEND key. It felt scarier than having the people at the workshop read and critique his writing. He felt exposed. *Too late now.* He would get back to work on the novel and try not to think about it.

Like that was going to happen.

Days went by. Finally, the woman at the adoption agency called him just as he was leaving for work at the library one morning.

"Avery? We've been processing your inquiry, and I'm afraid I have some bad news for you. We found a match for your date, but the birth mother has marked the records as closed. We aren't allowed to share them."

Avery's heart sank. As anxious as he was about the possibility of finally meeting his birth mother, having that option taken away was like a door slamming in his face.

"Isn't there anything I can do?"

"Some people have had success with lawsuits, but even if you do find her that way, she might not be receptive. Since she doesn't have the file marked open, she apparently hasn't started a search from her end. You might be setting yourself up for more pain. But of course that's completely up to you."

Brokenhearted and confused, Avery's first impulse was to speak with Julia, but he was actually kind of mad at her. But he also felt that she really cared about what happened to him—until she didn't show up for the Sunday morning panel at the workshop. *What was that about?*

He found her business card in his backpack and stared at her cell phone number. *Call or text?* A text would be safer, in case she didn't want to talk to him.

Hi. Julia. It's me, Avery, from the workshop. Can you chat?

He waited a few minutes. No reply. But as he put his phone in his pocket, he felt it vibrate.

Hello Avery. Sure. What's up?

He took a deep breath before typing his reply.

Can you meet me for a cup of coffee? I've got some difficult news and could really use someone to talk to.

Oh, sure. I've got a break after my class tomorrow morning. Meet you at Uptown Coffee around 10:30?

That would be great. Thanks. See you then.

Avery worked extra hours at the library that day. When his boss asked why he was still there two hours after his shift, he said he had been wanting to reorganize the children's section since the children's librarian had been out sick for a few days. Not really a lie, since he loved children's books and wanted their space to be welcoming. Some of his fondest childhood memories involved hours spent poring through library books while his brother was out playing ball.

After a restless night, it was finally the next morning. He arrived at the coffee shop a few minutes early and ordered their house brand, black, and found a seat in the corner, where they would have a little more privacy. Julia walked in and waved at him from the front door before ordering a cappuccino, which she brought with her to the table.

"Good morning. It's so good to see you again, Avery," she said warmly.

"Hi. Thanks for meeting me. I wasn't sure if you would."

"Why not?"

"Because you didn't show up the last day of the workshop, and Grant couldn't really explain why. I wanted to call you that day, but I didn't want to intrude."

"I see. I think I told Grant that I was late on a deadline for a manuscript that was due to my agent, or something like that."

"Yeah, that's what he said. But is that really true?"

"Wow. You get right to it, don't you?" Julia shifted in her chair and sipped her cappuccino nervously.

"I'm sorry. I guess it's none of my business. Or maybe I'm trying to deflect my concerns onto you, since I've got something difficult to talk to you about."

Julia looked relieved and eager to shift the focus onto Avery. "Sure. Is something wrong?"

"Yeah, you could say that. Remember when we had lunch that day and Adele encouraged me to search for my birth mother?"

Julia nodded.

"Well, I did. And the agency where my parents adopted me said they couldn't give me any information about her, because she had marked the files as closed. When I asked what that meant, they said it meant she didn't want to be found, basically. They said that birth mothers who want to be found usually initiate a search from their end, and she hadn't done that."

Julia took a deep breath, uncrossed her legs, and leaned her elbows on the table, resting her forehead on her clasped hands. Finally, she looked up and their eyes met.

"When were you born?"

"What? Oh, in 1992."

"Okay. What day?"

"June 30."

"And where were you born?"

"My adoption records list the University Hospital in Jackson, so I guess that's where. Why are you asking all these questions?"

Julia sat back in her chair and looked out the window. It was a pretty day, but there weren't many people in the chairs on the patio.

"Okay with you if we go outside? Where it's more private?'

Avery shrugged. "Sure, let's go."

They found a table in the shade along the outside wall of the building.

"So, that day I didn't show up for the workshop panel, I didn't have a deadline on a manuscript. I just didn't want to see you again."

"Why? Did I do something to upset you?"

"No, of course not. It's just that—well, I didn't know what was going on then, but now I'm pretty sure." She took a deep breath and wiped her eyes with a napkin from the table. "Here's the thing, Avery. When I was fifteen, I had a huge crush on a senior at my high school. He was tall, handsome, and real smart—editor of the school newspaper. And he was going away to college the next year. I was just a freshman, but I was working on the newspaper staff, writing feature stories, selling advertising, anything they'd let me do.

"Well, one afternoon we were working in the journalism room after school and he asked me out. I was floored. He usually only dated girls his age. That weekend I went with him to a football game, and afterwards I lost my virginity to him in the back seat of his car. It was September 30. The beginning of the school year, and I wondered what this might mean for us. Would he keep dating me, or was he just using me?"

Avery shifted in his chair, tossed his hair back, giving Julia a better view of his light-brown eyes, and folded his hands in his lap. He never took his eyes off Julia. "So, why are you telling me this?"

Julia stood and turned away from Avery, facing the opening at the back of the patio. Taking a deep breath, she turned back around. She was crying and could barely speak through her tears. "Because nine months later I had a baby. On June 30, 1992, at University Hospital in Jackson. I was sixteen and unmarried, so I gave . . . the baby up for adoption."

Avery jumped up from his chair, putting him face-to-face with Julia. He matched her tears with a flood of his own. He wanted to jump over the table and give her a big hug, but caution froze him.

"So, does this mean what I think it means? Are you saying that you could be my birth mother?"

"Yes. I mean, I think there are too many coincidences here. But we'll know for sure once I call the children's home and change the file status from closed to open."

"Do you want to do that? I mean, what do you want all of this to mean?"

"I want to call them right away, before we both get our hopes up too much."

"Our hopes? Does that mean you've changed your mind?"

"Yes! Before I met you, the baby—my son—was just an abstract being. And one I thought I could forget about one day. But the guilt never went away. And the shame for what happened when I was fifteen. But now, I'm looking at an amazing young man who just might have my DNA, and I couldn't be more hopeful."

They shared another hug and a rush of more tears. A few more customers found their way from the coffee shop out to the patio, but Julia and Avery didn't care about privacy anymore. They were both eager for the next chapter of their lives to begin, and they headed to Julia's house to make that phone call.

Sitting in her den with Avery, as awkward as two teenagers on a first date, Julia called the children's home. Avery could only hear her end of the call.

"Yes, this is Julia Wilson. I'm in your database as a birth mother from 1992. My files have been closed since then, but I'd like to change that now. What? Can't I just do it over the phone? Oh, I understand. Email the form and I'll get it notarized and send it back today. Why today? I've met a young man I believe might be my birth son. He inquired with you recently. His name is Avery Carmichael. Date of birth June 30, 1992. We're anxious to know if our files match. He's here with me now. Okay, thank you."

She looked at Avery and took a deep breath. "I guess you got the gist of that. I've got to download this legal form and sign it and get it notarized before she can open my file and tell us what we want to know."

Avery was pacing the room. "Can I come with you?"

"What about your job?"

"I'm off today. And besides, this is more important!"

Julia printed off the form, and they were out the door and off to a mail center to get it notarized. Back home less than an hour later, she scanned the form and emailed it back to the children's home. A few minutes later her cell rang.

"Yes? You got the form? Good. What's next?" Julia and Avery were sitting at a table in her study, near her computer and printer. Suddenly Julia jumped up and screamed, "Yes! Thank you so much! He's here with me now! I'll tell him."

Avery waited to hear the words.

"It's confirmed. You're my son! They want you to contact them to officially close out your search for your birth mother."

Avery stood quietly holding his mother in his arms. He still had so many questions—especially about his biological father—but they could wait. For now, he was anxious to nurture this new relationship. And to get back to his book, where Balock and Ember were still searching for their parents. It was pretty obvious where that story would end.

Back home in Memphis, I was thrilled to get a phone call from Avery, telling me the news of his discovery and his growing relationship with his birth mother. But then we lost touch for a year or two. And then one day I was searching the internet for literary events and came across a notice on Square Books' calendar for a reading and signing coming up the next month. Avery Carmichael would be reading from his debut dystopian fantasy novel, *The Orphan Rebellion*. I marked the date on my calendar. This was one literary event I wasn't going to miss!

SENATOBIA

John and Mary Margaret

When I pulled into the parking lot at Northwest Mississippi Community College's R. C. Pugh Library in Senatobia, Mississippi, I felt like I was still in Memphis. It was only forty miles from my house to the venue of the library book club's monthly meeting. I would be talking with this group about my memoir, which tells the story of my mother's decline with Alzheimer's and how it changed our relationship. Members of Pugh's reading roundtable received copies of the visiting author's books for just five dollars, thanks to a grant from Sycamore Bank. I love how my home state supports reading.

My mother died from Alzheimer's in May 2016. I never actually took care of her in my home or hers since she was in a nursing home in Jackson, Mississippi, for the last eight years of her life. But I made the 400-mile round-trip to visit her once or twice a month for most of those years, and handled her finances and medical and legal paperwork.

The emotional and spiritual aspects of being her caregiver fell to me because my father died in 1998. When my mother started showing signs of dementia a few years later, I sold her house and moved her into an assisted living facility.

Once she adjusted, she was happy there for about three years. But then she broke her hip, and after a few days in the hospital for surgery and a few weeks in a nursing home for rehab, it became clear that she could never return to assisted living. When she entered a nursing home in 2008, we didn't know she would live another eight years, enduring a slow and awful decline as tangles and plaques suffocated her brain cells.

I hoped the folks of Senatobia wouldn't be too depressed by my story and that they would share some of their own. Alzheimer's disease leaves in its wake communities of caregivers tested emotionally and physically.

As I entered the meeting room at the Senatobia library, I was greeted by Sharon, the group's organizer, and a room full of mostly women, which I've found to be the case with many of these book groups.

"We're so glad you're here. Would you like some coffee or water or a soft drink?"

"Hi, Sharon. Some water would be great, thanks."

I looked around at the group of about twenty people. As I was about to sit and begin the discussion, an elderly couple entered and found two seats near the front. *Why do people always leave the front row empty?* I introduced myself and offered my hand, first to the woman. Her eyes twinkled as they met mine.

"Hello, I'm Mary Margaret Sutherland."

"Welcome, Mary Margaret. And who is this handsome gentleman?"

He offered his hand. "John Abbott. Nice to meet you."

They appeared to be in their mid-seventies and were so attractive that it was difficult to tell. John was African American, and his mostly gray hair was cropped short. He wore a light denim shirt, a houndstooth sports jacket, and starched jeans topping off a pair of cowboy boots, and he looked to be about six foot two. Tortoiseshell glasses framed his chocolate eyes, which seemed to find their way to Mary Margaret as often as possible.

Mary Margaret's slim physique was modestly adorned with black slacks and a winter white shell and cardigan that looked like Eileen Fisher. Her hair was blond with a touch of silver, and was pulled back into a low, messy side bun. Beautiful diamond studs garnished her ears. My eyes followed their shine down her right arm to find a matching tennis bracelet. She had a copy of my book tucked under one arm and held John's hand with her other one. A pebbled, black leather Coach cross-body clutch hung at her side. They both spoke or nodded to others sitting near them, and everyone settled down for the discussion.

I wasn't surprised that several people in the group were currently caregivers for a spouse or parent with Alzheimer's or other debilitating illnesses. And some had already lost the loved one they cared for.

As we discussed the various stages I wrote about in my book— my mother's failing health and the transitions from independent living to assisted living to nursing home care—I asked if anyone in the group currently had a loved one who was in a nursing home. John and Mary Margaret were among those who raised their hands.

We talked about the difficulty of letting go, and especially how painful it was when the loved one no longer recognized us when we visited. A few people in the group shared personal stories. John and Mary Margaret remained still and quiet, seemingly soaking in others' tribulations while contemplating their own. After the meeting I approached them and asked if they would like to have a cup of coffee with me.

"I'd really love to hear more about your personal journeys as caregivers, if you don't mind sharing."

They looked at each other for a moment; Mary Margaret nodded, and John replied, "Sure. We live a few minutes from here. Would you like to come to our house?"

I was surprised by the invitation but gladly accepted and put their address into my GPS. After signing a few books and thanking Sharon for hosting me, I made the short drive through a wooded subdivision to their home.

It was a lovely one-story French stucco house in a quiet cul-de-sac. John and Mary Margaret were inside when I arrived, and John met me at the door. He escorted me into the kitchen where Mary Margaret was putting on a pot of coffee and setting out cups and a plate of egg salad sandwiches, cut into finger-sized servings. They moved comfortably around each other—like a couple that had been together for many years. We sat at the breakfast table and after a few quiet moments, I broke the silence.

"So, you didn't share any of your stories at the meeting. I'm very interested to know more about your loved ones who are in a nursing home, or what your situation is. Do both of you have a parent with Alzheimer's?"

They smiled softly, first at me and then at one another. John nodded at Mary Margaret, who began their story.

"I guess I'll begin at the beginning."

Something about her expression and tone made me think there was more to their story than caregiving for an elderly parent.

"John and I were sweethearts at Ole Miss, back in the 1960s."

John had been a star football player at George Washington Carver, an all-black high school in Memphis. He had invitations to play ball at a traditionally black college, but he gave up those dreams in order to attend Ole Miss. In the mid-sixties, blacks weren't allowed to play football at the segregated university. The first to do so was Robert "Gentle Ben" Williams in 1972.

"I want to study law, not get bruised and battered on a football field," John told his father.

"But you could get a full scholarship if you play ball at Jackson State," his father argued. "And be with your own people. At Ole Miss you're going to be a minority and no telling what all that will mean."

John eventually won the argument and headed to Oxford, Mississippi, as a freshman in 1966.

John kept to himself for a good bit of his freshman, sophomore, and junior years, but in 1969 he met Mary Margaret in a survey of American literature class. He was struck by her beauty but also her love for the written word. And surprisingly, she made the first move.

"Would you like to study together for the Faulkner exam?" Her blue eyes twinkled, and her blond ponytail shone in the sunshine as they walked outside after class one day.

"Sure. We could grab some lunch at the union and study there, or over at the grove since it's so pretty outside today." John's heart raced as he anticipated spending time with Mary Margaret outside class.

"Well—" Mary Margaret paused, choosing her next words carefully. "I eat at the house—the Tri Delt house—but I could meet you at the grove around one thirty. Or you could come over to the house and we could study there."

"Are you sure that would be okay?" John looked at the ground and shuffled his feet nervously. Somehow the thought of a black boy inside a white sorority house on the Ole Miss campus conjured up images of white-jacketed black waiters at a country club. "Are blacks even allowed in there as guests?"

"I—I haven't ever thought about it," Mary Margaret said.

"Well, have you ever seen any black students at your sorority house?" John persisted.

"No, I guess not. But it's high time that changed. Boys aren't allowed for meals, but why don't you come on over after lunch and we'll study in the living room."

John was nervous as a cat as he walked down Sorority Row and stopped at the door to the Delta Delta Delta house, with its historic redbrick walls and stately white columns. *Should I knock?* Just as he was deciding, a pretty young coed came up the steps behind him and said, "Deliveries are around back."

"Oh, no, I'm not delivering anything. I'm here to see Mary Margaret—I mean, Miss Sutherland. We're going to study together."

The girl stared at him in disbelief. After a moment of silence she replied, "Oh, I see. Well, come in then."

John followed her into the foyer where girls were coming and going from lunch in the dining room, some scurrying up the staircase to their sleeping quarters. A middle-aged woman dressed in a polyester knit suit approached John.

"May I help you?"

"Yes, ma'am. I'm John Abbott. I'm here to study with Mary Margaret Sutherland. We have literature class together." He looked nervously around, wishing he and Mary Margaret had made plans to study at the grove or the library—anywhere but here! Just then, Mary Margaret came into the foyer.

"Oh, there you are, John. I see you've met Mrs. Murray, our house mother."

"We haven't formally met, but John was just telling me he's here to study with you. Is that true?" Mrs. Murray's eyes remained fixed on John's, even as she addressed her question to Mary Margaret.

"Yes, ma'am. We've got an American lit exam coming up."

Mary Margaret smiled nonchalantly at John and Mrs. Murray, swinging her ponytail confidently as she moved towards the stairs.

"I'll be right back down, John. I've got to run upstairs and get my notes. Mrs. Murray will show you into the living room."

Mrs. Murray silently led John into the well-appointed living area, where several other girls were already ensconced in the overstuffed chairs and sofas, textbooks and pen and papers spread out around them. "Y'all can work over there." She pointed to a small square table with four chairs.

"Thank you."

John settled into one of the chairs and opened his notebook to the pages where he had recorded several potential discussion questions on Faulkner's *The Sound and the Fury.* Several pairs of eyes watched as he tried to concentrate on the words in front of him. Finally, Mary Margaret joined him at the table.

"Ready to get started?" she asked without a hint of discomfort.

"I guess so. Your house mother didn't seem too happy to see me here, though."

"Oh, she'll get over it. There's a first time for everything. Like Dylan said, 'Times they are a-changin'.'"

John and Mary Margaret studied together that afternoon, and several more in the coming weeks. Their love for Southern literature seemed to morph seamlessly into a mutual attraction, and finally John got up the courage to ask her for a date to an upcoming football game.

"I'd love to! Drop by the house around seven and we'll walk to the stadium together."

Saturday night arrived and John waited anxiously for Mary Margaret in the foyer at the house. She came downstairs amidst the flutter of a houseful of sorority sisters heading out the door with their dates, greeting him with a hug and her characteristic dimpled smile.

Outside on the sidewalk headed towards the stadium, someone yelled at John from the street, "Hey, you! What do you think you're doing, *boy*?"

Mary Margaret and John stopped walking and looked around at Mary Margaret's friends and their dates, who were also stopped in their tracks by the outburst.

"Just ignore him; he's an idiot!" Mary Margaret said, grabbing John's hand.

The crowd thickened as they entered the stadium and found their seats accompanied by quite a few stares but no verbal or physical attacks. As the excitement of the ballgame heated up, everyone seemed to forget about the daring biracial couple. Ole Miss beat Vanderbilt that night, and the campus erupted with school spirit as students poured out of the stadium and into the fraternity houses for the after-game parties. As John and Mary Margaret returned to the Tri Delt house, he asked if she'd like to go somewhere to celebrate. Since there were no black fraternities on campus, they were like a couple without a country.

Mary Margaret felt the loneliness of their predicament as her sorority sisters headed to parties with their dates. John had a 1959 Chevrolet Bel Air—a gift from his parents. They climbed into the front seat and sat looking at each other expectantly.

"I guess we should have talked about what to do after the game," John offered.

"It's not like I didn't think about it," Mary Margaret said. "But I didn't want to bring it up . . . to make you feel bad or anything."

After an awkward silence, John said, "Do you like the blues?"

"Music? Oh, I guess that sounded stupid! I'm not sure. I mean, most of the music we have at parties on campus now is either rock and roll or Motown. Why?"

"Well, there's a band called the Checkmates that plays out at a club on Old Sardis Road. Are you up for a different kind of cultural experience? You will probably be the only white person there."

Mary Margaret held her hand across her abdomen to calm the growing knot. "I guess so. But we have to be back by midnight for curfew at the house."

"Of course."

Forty-five minutes later they pulled into the gravel parking lot at Tom Charlie's. John opened the door for Mary Margaret.

As they entered the smoke-filled club, lead singer Henry Cook was just getting warmed up on stage, and the all-black audience mingled at the bar and small tables scattered around the stage. All eyes were trained on Mary Margaret as John led her to a corner table.

He settled her into a chair before asking what she'd like to drink.

"I'll have a Coke."

"You sure that's all you want? They don't check IDs here."

"Yeah, I'm sure."

John went to the bar to get their drinks while Mary Margaret nervously twirled a blond curl that had escaped her barrette. Most of the couples staring as she and John walked in had gone back to watching the stage from their tables or moving rhythmically on the dance floor. John quickly returned with their drinks and smiled as he watched Mary Margaret absorb the scene.

"You're not in Kansas anymore," he said.

She laughed. "Okay, I've never heard music like this before. I like it, but I admit that it feels weird in here. How do you ever get used to being in the minority?"

"To be honest, I don't get used to it. I'd like to be part of changing the culture, but there's a lot of history behind the way things are, especially in the South."

"You ever thought of moving away?"

"Not really. I'd rather stay and try to make things better. I'd like to go to law school and work as a public defender in Memphis one day. Or maybe somewhere in Mississippi."

"Wow. You are dreaming big."

"Why do you say that? You mean because I'm a Negro?"

"Okay, I can see how that sounded racist. But what I meant was that's a big goal for any college student, not just because of your race."

"What about your goals? With your love for Southern writers, are you going to become a writer yourself?"

Mary Margaret laughed. "Hardly. I'll teach school. Hopefully get married and have kids. Of course, my folks want me to settle in Jackson, where I grew up."

"That all sounds so idyllic, and safe."

Mary Margaret let John's words settle as she sipped her Coke. The blues soothed her, floating through the room and into her heart.

The two sat for more than an hour, relaxed and content. Suddenly, she noticed it was eleven o'clock.

"We've got to go or I'll miss curfew!"

Mary Margaret moved closer to John on the front seat as he started the engine. "I'm really glad you brought me here, John."

Their eyes found each other's through the dim lights from the club, and John leaned down. The kiss was tender but also shocking. Mary Margaret moved reluctantly back across the seat, and John drove out of the parking lot.

They were both quiet on the ride back to campus, and when they pulled up in front of the Tri Delt house groups of kids were everywhere. As John opened the car door for Mary Margaret, several couples approached. One of their dates yelled at John.

"What do you think you're doing, *boy*?"

Before John could answer, the antagonist punched John's face.

Mary Margaret jumped from the car and screamed as she knelt down to help John, who was bleeding from the nose and mouth. She looked at the boy who had hit him, a junior basketball player named Jimbo.

"Are you crazy? He wasn't doing anything wrong, you racist pig!"

By then a crowd had gathered, and a few other boys pulled Jimbo away from the sidewalk and the couples began moving towards the house.

"Are you okay?" Mary Margaret asked as she helped John to his feet.

"Yeah, I'm fine. But I think you might want to head on inside by yourself. I don't want to cause you any more embarrassment. I guess I'll see you in class next week."

Mary Margaret wanted to argue with him. To tell him to walk her to the door like the other boys were doing with their dates. To reassure him that they could hang out together and everything would be fine. But she knew that wasn't true. Tears filed her eyes as she watched John drive off.

John and Mary Margaret only saw each other in lit class for the rest of the semester, and once they returned from Christmas break, they continued with their separate lives on campus. Mary Margaret practice taught at a local high school that spring and began dating a senior named Walter. She wore his Sigma Chi pin and hoped for a ring before graduation.

John got involved with the Black Student Union (BSU) in February, joining a group of black students who danced on tables in the cafeteria to the music of Mississippi bluesman B. B. King one night, stormed the stage during a concert at Fulton Chapel the next day, and marched to the home of Chancellor Porter Fortune, who ironically had permitted the formation of the BSU to provide black students with a venue for expressing their concerns about the acts of harassment.

Mary Margaret and Walter got married the following year and ended up living in Memphis, where she taught English at Hutchinson, a private girls' school. John stayed in Oxford and finished at the law school four years later. He moved to Memphis—where he met and married a woman named Elizabeth—to work as a public defender for Shelby County, seeking legal and social justice for those unable to afford it, often members of the African-American community.

Although both couples lived in Memphis and raised their children there, John and Mary Margaret never ran into each other for about fifty years. And then fate dealt them an interesting blow.

As we sipped coffee and ate sandwiches, John and Mary Margaret took turns filling in the years for me. John and his wife had two boys. They raised them in a fairly diverse neighborhood in Midtown, sending them to public schools. Mary Margaret's family lived in East Memphis, near her husband's insurance agency, and their three children attended private schools. Once all the kids were grown—Mary Margaret and John shared a dozen grandchildren between them by the time they were in their sixties—both couples retired and moved the short distance south of Memphis to Senatobia, Mississippi, where housing was more affordable and crime was less rampant. They thought they were moving towards their sunset years with their spouses of several decades.

"Elizabeth—my wife—and Mary Margaret's husband, Walter, both had fairly early onset Alzheimer's and began declining quickly. I kept Elizabeth at home with me as long as I could, but once her care became more than I could handle, I moved her into a nursing home."

"I had a similar experience with Walter. Sometime last year John and I ran into each other at the nursing home where Walter and Elizabeth are both residents. You can imagine our shock in seeing each other after so many years."

John smiled. "I would have known Mary Margaret anywhere. Those same sparkling baby blue eyes and dimpled smile."

Mary Margaret blushed the way only true Southern women do at the simplest compliment.

"When John hugged me in the lobby of the nursing home, I felt those old feelings from that one kiss back on the Ole Miss campus come crashing into my heart all over again. I felt as silly as a schoolgirl. And then I remembered that my Walter was right down the hall."

"At that point, neither Elizabeth nor Walter knew who we were anymore. Sure, they might smile when we entered the room, but in the same way they would acknowledge the presence of any visitor," John said.

"We were both visiting them daily, and once we discovered that we lived near each other, we began riding to and from the nursing home together most days," Mary Margaret added. "On days that were especially difficult emotionally, we would often stop somewhere for dinner and a glass of wine after we left the nursing home . . . and sometimes a cry. It was wonderful to have each other's support as we were losing our life partners. But then we realized that the old spark from our college days was being reignited. It was confusing. We both loved our spouses, but they weren't really there anymore."

John reached for Mary Margaret's hand, patted it with his other hand, and then handed her a handkerchief. As she wiped her tears, he continued the story.

"Our children had moved away, some out west and some up to the northeast, so it was just us at this point. And although we both have fairly good retirement incomes, the nursing home care eats through those dollars pretty quickly. We needed to do something, and we didn't want to end up on Medicaid. So we sold my house and I moved in with Mary Margaret about six months ago. The money from the sale should cover the nursing home expenses for a few years."

Mary Margaret blushed as John said those words. I rushed to reassure her.

"How wonderful! Not only that you found a helpful solution, but also that you found each other after all these years."

"Well," Mary Margaret said as she recovered her composure, "it's not like we're living in sin or anything. We each have our own bedroom. But our children are a bit scandalized by it. And some of our friends at church."

"Oh, I'm sure your children are just sad for the loss of the relationships they knew all their lives. They'll come around. And those people at church—well, you do still live in Mississippi, so there will probably always be some of that! Although I'm more surprised that they aren't more concerned about you being a mixed-race couple."

"Yes," John answered, "I think there's some of that, too. But mostly my kids think I'm being unfaithful to their mother. And Mary Margaret's children feel that she's cheating on their father, emotionally, if not physically."

"Have you talked about this with any of your friends, like others in the book club?"

"At a meeting a few months ago we were discussing Nicholas Sparks' book *The Notebook* on its twentieth anniversary," Mary Margaret said. "Everyone seemed to be so impressed with how Noah stayed in the institution with his wife, Allie, even when she no longer knew who he was, and even though their children encouraged him to move on with his life."

"There were mixed feelings about how he took both of their lives in the end," John said. "But many in the group even applauded that. Mary Margaret and I became quiet at book club after that meeting. We've even considered not going anymore, but we don't have many social opportunities. We don't like to drive to Memphis at night to visit old friends there, so we spend most of our evenings at home, just the two of us."

"What about your days?" I asked, eager to know more about their lives at this crucial juncture.

"Oh, we visit Walter and Elizabeth every day," Mary Margaret said. John smiled and nodded. "We usually head over to the nursing home around ten and spend a couple of hours, usually visiting in the lobby. Sometimes we stay for lunch with them in the dining room, but sometimes we treat ourselves to pizza at Buon Cibo or a sandwich at the Burger Shop."

"And your afternoons?"

"If we're not too tired"—John looked at Mary Margaret—"sometimes we drive into Memphis and visit the Brooks Museum of Art or the Dixon, or take in a matinee at one of the movie theaters."

"I've got arthritis," Mary Margaret said, "so sometimes we just come back here to the house and rest. We might take a nap, or read, or even get on our computers and look for pictures of our kids on Facebook or Instagram."

"Mary Margaret's being humble now," John interjected. "She's also writing a book."

"Oh, really? What's it about?" I leaned across the table in anticipation of her answer.

"It's a novel." Mary Margaret clasped her hands together on the table and moved them to her lap, looking down as she did.

"Go on, tell her about it," John coaxed.

"Well, it's about a mixed-race couple who fall in love at a mostly white college—in the South."

SOUTHAVEN

Shelby

S outhaven, Mississippi, feels very much like a suburb of its neighbor, Memphis, fifteen miles north, but with enough small-town charm to keep plenty of commuters within its borders. It's especially popular with folks who work in Downtown Memphis.

Since I live right on the Mississippi River in Harbor Town, Southaven is a quicker drive for me than the closest Target store or shopping mall in East Memphis. Four miles from the Memphis International Airport, and with 50,000 residents, it's the third largest city in Mississippi—coming in after Jackson and Gulfport. Southaven boasts a plethora of shopping outlets and antique stores. The Landers Civic Center shines with its luxury suites, a convention hall, a theater for the performing arts and a sporting arena. Dale's family-owned country restaurant rivals chains like Cracker Barrel, and Southaven boasts its own Gus's World Famous Fried Chicken.

Among the town's treasures is the M. R. Davis Library, which is part of the First Regional Library cooperative, with fourteen branch locations in Desoto, Lafayette, Panola, Tate, and Tunica Counties in northern Mississippi. The libraries I visited in Oxford and Senatobia are also part of this organization, and they are all shining lights of the state's literary heritage. Once I saw a highway billboard sponsored by the Mississippi Believe It! campaign that read, *Yes, we can read. A few of us can even write.*

Indeed, we can. Mississippi boasts more honored and revered writers than any other state in the nation, including more than a dozen Pulitzer Prize winners and finalists.

It was in this rich literary milieu that I found myself on a beautiful spring day, having been invited to speak to the Southaven library's book club. Outside the library, a brilliant Japanese cherry blossom tree was in full bloom, signaling the start of another colorful season in this town in the northwestern-most corner of Mississippi. Unlike the groups in smaller towns throughout the state, the crowd in Southaven that day included quite a few younger folks, like the librarian who was hosting me for this visit. She greeted me cheerfully when I entered the library.

"Hello, Mrs. Covington. I'm Nora Richardson. We've been emailing. I'm so glad you could join us today! We're just getting refreshments and chairs set up in the back room. Follow me."

"Thank you, but please call me Adele. I'm so happy to be here. I didn't realize how close the library was to my house. It's actually closer than the main library in Memphis."

The library was larger than I had expected, and spacious, with lots of windows for light. I imagined its patrons enjoying hours within its walls, reading for pleasure, researching, even writing a book.

After the group gathered and got coffee and pastries, I made my way to the front of the room. I read from and discussed my novel and its protagonist, a young girl named Mare, who suffers childhood sexual abuse, escapes from a religious cult, and throws up graffiti to try to get her message out to the public. She is eventually discovered by a photographer for *Rolling Stone,* mentored by a famous abstract expressionist painter, and seeks answers to some of life's mysteries from a nun. In one scene, when she is visiting an Orthodox monastery to learn to paint icons, she encounters one that is weeping. She becomes so overwhelmed that she passes out. Another icon weeps in the final chapter of the book, at an art show to raise money for a women's shelter.

Nora was the first person to raise her hand during the question and answer time.

"Adele, please tell us more about the weeping icons in your novel. I know it's a fiction story, but are they real? I mean, do they really happen? And what does it mean?"

"Those are very good questions. Before I wrote this novel, I made numerous visits to Orthodox monasteries, including several trips to participate in icon-painting workshops. On one of those trips I went with several of the nuns to a church in a nearby town to see some weeping icons. And while I didn't faint the first time I witnessed this miracle, like Mare does in the book, the experience had a huge impact on me."

"The first time? So, did you see more of these icons another time?" Nora asked.

"Yes. I went to Chicago with three friends from my church on a pilgrimage to see weeping icons in three different churches there. At one church there was this woman who had traveled a long distance to see the icon and pray before it. She knelt at the back of the nave and *walked on her knees* all the way down the aisle before prostrating herself in front of the icon. She was praying in another language the whole time, so I don't know what she was saying, but she was crying and obviously moved by the icon."

The room went silent until another woman asked, "But what does it *mean*, when the icon weeps?"

I took a deep breath. "Most weeping icons are of the Mother of God, and some theologians say that she—through the vehicle of her image in the icon—is weeping because she is sad, because she is grieving over something. Probably the state of the world in general, and maybe someone's pain specifically. Many people go on pilgrimages to venerate these icons, hoping for healing for themselves or someone they love."

Nora raised her hand again. "What happens when people venerate a weeping icon?"

"Often a priest is there, and he takes a bit of the tears—which look like oil and smell like sweet myrrh—on a small cotton ball or sometimes using a paintbrush, and anoints the worshipers with it, on their forehead and hands, saying something like, 'For the healing of soul and body.' And sometimes they will give you a piece of the cotton that has been dipped in the oil to take home with you, in a small airtight container like a Ziploc baggie. You can then use it to anoint yourself or others."

Nora's eyes filled with tears as she asked, "So, these tears can heal people? Has this ever been proven?"

"Many times. You can find documented accounts in various places, including online. But it's not magic any more than prayer is magic. Faith is involved. And not everyone who prays before a weeping icon is healed. God's ways are mysterious." I paused for a moment and then asked, "Are there any other questions about the novel?"

The room fell quiet again, and I noticed another woman had her arm around Nora's shoulder. I thanked the group for inviting me and moved to the table in the back of the room to sign books. After everyone left, Nora approached me.

"Thanks so much for coming and sharing with us today. I'm sorry if I dominated the discussion and let my personal emotions get in the way."

"Oh, not at all. It's an emotional book."

"I know, but there are so many other interesting scenes in the book about graffiti and abstract art, and we didn't really have time to talk much about that."

"It's really okay, Nora. I've done readings at many libraries and bookstores and book clubs for this book, and the discussion is always unique and organic. I don't try to guide it in any direction. I was interested, though, in how passionate you were about the weeping icons. Is this more than a literary curiosity?"

Nora nodded. "My daughter has cancer, a rare form of leukemia that actually is a combination of two types. It's called *mixed phenotype*. It's much harder to treat than either the myeloid or the lymphoblastic types are on their own. She's been treated at St. Jude in Memphis on and off for several years." Her eyes filled with tears again, which she brushed aside, and she started cleaning up from the meeting.

"Oh, Nora, I'm so sorry. How old is she?"

"Shelby is seven. She was diagnosed about four years ago and has been in and out of the hospital many times for chemo, radiation, even a stem cell transplant."

Nora moved around the room as she spoke, straightening chairs and throwing away the used coffee cups and napkins. I stopped her and we sat.

"You know, I live about three minutes from St. Jude. If you or your husband ever need a place to stay or if I can do anything to help . . ." I offered, trying to think of something encouraging to say.

"That's so nice, but we only live about fifteen minutes away, and we usually take turns being with Shelby when she's in the hospital. My husband is a computer software consultant. He works from home and can even work from the hospital room when he needs to. And the library has been great about letting me keep a flexible schedule." She paused for a moment, and then added, "But there might be something you can do for us." She looked into my eyes.

"Sure. Anything." I reached over and touched her hand, squeezing it slightly.

"Since I first read your book, I've had the desire to take Shelby to see a weeping icon. For her to be anointed with the holy oil—the tears. We're not Orthodox, and I'm sure our friends in our Baptist church would be scandalized, since they pretty much believe that venerating icons is like worshipping idols, but this is something I really want to do. Can you help me find one?"

"Oh, wow. I wasn't expecting that. What would your husband say?"

"He's not very religious, actually. We were married in the Baptist church because that's where I grew up. But he wouldn't be opposed to it. He loves Shelby and would do anything to help her. Her prognosis isn't very good. There's only a fifty to sixty percent chance she will live more than five years past her diagnosis, and she's already four years in."

Her words sank in as my thoughts flew back to my experiences with weeping icons.

"It's been over twenty years since I saw those weeping icons, but I can ask my pastor if he knows where the closest one might be these days. We can probably get some information online, but I'd rather ask him personally. He might even call our bishop for advice."

Nora choked up again. "That would be"—she paused to swallow—"that would be amazing. You've got my phone and email."

Back home I called my pastor, Father Andrew, and told him Shelby's situation. "I'll ask the bishop for a suggestion," he said. "I've never actually seen a weeping icon in person, but I'm sure he will know of one, and can tell us which one is closest. How far can Shelby travel?"

"I didn't ask. I think she's in remission now, since her mother didn't mention travel being a problem."

The next day Father Andrew called me back to tell me about a miracle-working icon that was currently weeping.

"Unfortunately, it's in Pennsylvania. I hope she can travel that far."

"Tell me more," I said.

"They are calling it 'the Tender Heart.' It's a myrrh-flowing icon of the Virgin Mary, and several people have been healed by its tears, including a woman with stage four cancer. Her doctor at Sloan Kettering Cancer Center told her that there was nothing he could do for her except control her pain. A friend anointed her with the myrrh and she was miraculously healed. Her doctor confirmed that there is no trace of the cancer, and that her healing can only be the result of a miracle."

"Oh my. Is the icon in an Orthodox church?"

"Yes, it's at Saint George in Taylor, Pennsylvania. I spoke with the priest there, and they welcome visitors. In fact, they pray a special service to the Mother of God every Wednesday night in front of the icon. People have also been healed from prostate cancer, liver cancer, throat cancer, lung cancer, brain lymphoma, and other illnesses."

"Wonderful! Maybe I can go with Nora and her family. I'd love to see this icon myself. I'll let her know the news. Thanks so much for your help."

I called Nora right away and told her about the icon in Pennsylvania.

"Would it be all right if I went with your family? I'd love to venerate this icon myself."

"Oh—yes! I'd love for you to come with us. We'll book our flights right away and I'll send you an email showing you which flight. Maybe you can travel with us, too."

I didn't hear back from Nora for two days. Worried that they were having problems with the airline schedules, I gave her another day before calling, and the call went right to voicemail. I left a message. Finally, four days after our conversation about visiting the icon together, she called me back.

"I'm so sorry I didn't call sooner, but I have some bad news."

"Oh no, what's wrong?"

"Shelby spiked a fever the night after you first called about the icon. She wouldn't eat, and bruises appeared again, which are usually a sign of internal bleeding. We rushed her to the hospital and have been here ever since. Her remission is over—the cancer has returned with a vengeance. The doctors say she is too sick to travel." Nora wept. "I'm devastated."

My heart sank and I searched for words, fighting back tears myself. "Maybe I can fly to Pennsylvania and bring back some of the tears for her."

"Oh, could you do that? I mean, would that even work? Or would she have to be in the presence of the icon itself?"

"The priest at the church where the icon is said that some people have been healed this way, so it's worth a try. I'll check the airline schedule today and get back with you."

"Please, hurry. She may not have much longer."

I hung up and immediately called Father Andrew with an update. He suggested that we visit Shelby and her parents at St. Jude together that afternoon.

"How will that help?" I asked.

"Well, I have an idea. But I will have to discuss it with her parents, and maybe also with her doctors. Can you meet me there, around three?"

"Of course. Her name is Shelby Richardson. Her parents are Nora and—oh, wait, I don't know the father's name."

"That's okay. I'm sure I can find her room with those names. I'll see you there."

When I walked into the lobby at St. Jude Children's Hospital, which is less than a half mile from my house, I was immediately taken by the children's artwork, which the staff—often dressed in silly costumes—rotate on the walls. The in-house design team makes sure there are happy, colorful images everywhere, creating an upbeat, hopeful atmosphere.

I found Shelby's room, where I was greeted by Nora and introduced for the first time to her husband, Mark. Shelby was in a coma, but Nora led me by the hand to her bedside, where I tried to hold my emotions in check. She was a tiny but beautiful little girl, pale from the disease. She had been intubated, and the only sound in the room was the hum of her ventilator.

Nora reached to adjust the flowered cap that covered her head.

"You should have seen her beautiful, chestnut hair, before she lost it."

"She's still beautiful." I put my arm around Nora, whose eyes were puffy.

"So, does the fact that you are here and not on a plane to Pennsylvania mean that you won't be able to bring tears from the icon for her?"

"I couldn't get a flight out until tomorrow. My priest said he wanted to meet me here first. He said he has an idea."

When Father Andrew entered, I introduced him to Nora and Mark. He walked over to Shelby's bed.

"Is it all right if I say a prayer for her?"

Mark shrugged. Nora answered, "Of course."

Father Andrew reached into his pocket and pulled out a small prayer book, from which he read the prayer for the sick:

"O Christ, Who alone art our Defender: Visit and heal Thy suffering servant Shelby, delivering her from sickness and grievous pains. Raise her up that she may sing to Thee and praise Thee without ceasing, through the prayers of the Theotokos, O Thou Who alone lovest mankind."

He made the sign of the cross over her and then turned to Nora and Mark.

"Thank you so much for allowing me to be here today. Adele has filled me in on Shelby's situation. I'm so sorry she isn't able to travel to Pennsylvania. I've spoken with the nurse at the station, and she has asked Nora's doctor to meet with us. He should be here any minute." He looked at his watch.

"Okay," Nora began, tentatively, "but how is this going to help heal Shelby?"

"We have a service every Friday night during Lent at our church in Midtown, just ten minutes from here. It's called the Akathist Hymn to the Mother of God. We set up an icon in the middle of the nave, and we chant prayers to the Mother of God, asking for her help, and praising her for her protection. I was hoping that you could bring Shelby tonight, which is why I asked to speak with her physician."

Nora and Mark looked at each other and then at Shelby.

"Is that icon weeping?" Nora asked.

"No, it isn't. But that doesn't mean that she doesn't hear our prayers."

"I can't imagine that they would let us move her, even for a ten-minute drive away, in her condition," Nora said.

"Yes, I can see that now," Father Andrew said. "I didn't realize that she was in a coma, or on a ventilator. But I have an alternative plan."

He reached into a bag that he had brought with him and pulled out an icon of the Mother of God, Queen of All—an image of the Virgin sitting on a throne, holding the Christ Child in her lap. He also pulled out an icon stand and set the icon up on a table near Shelby's bed.

"Would you mind if we prayed a special prayer with this icon?"

"Didn't you just pray for her?" Mark spoke for the first time. "Maybe you should just leave us alone so we can be alone with our daughter during what's probably going to be her last hours."

Nora looked at her husband and then the icon. "I don't see what it can hurt, Mark. Let him do the prayers. It won't take long, will it, Father?"

"This is a copy of a miracle-working icon known as the Mother of God, Queen of All, which has been known to cure people with cancer. We'll do a short version of a prayer called the Akathist of the Mother of God, Healer of Cancer."

I nodded and Nora moved closer to the bed, placing her hand on Shelby's. Mark joined her, and we all faced the icon as Father Andrew began the prayer. A few stanzas in, he chanted these words:

> You have done amazing things, O Place of God, by healing through Your Holy Icon. Accepting the streams of Your healing we sing, O Queen of All, the song of thanksgiving:
> Rejoice, the Medicine that reduces pain!
> Rejoice, the Coolness that cools fever of the ailments!
> Rejoice, You Who cauterize the illness of cancer like fire!

And near the end of the Akathist he prayed,

> O our Mother Queen of All, Who gave birth to the Word, Holiest of all Saints! Having accepted our singing today, heal us from every deadly illness and from the coming condemnation, save those who sing: Alleluia!

Just as Father Andrew finished, I closed my eyes and took a deep breath. I thought I smelled roses, but there weren't any flowers in Shelby's room. When I opened my eyes, Father Andrew had stopped praying and was staring intently at the icon. A liquid dripped from the Mother of God's eyes onto the table.

"Quick! Get a bowl! A cup! Anything!"

Before I could move, Nora grabbed a plastic cup from the table by Shelby's bed and handed it to Father Andrew. He held it under the icon, and the liquid continued to drip into the cup. "Get something to raise the icon up higher so I can place the cup at its base."

I looked around and found some Kleenex boxes and stacked them under the icon. Father Andrew placed the cup at its base.

"What is that?" Nora said. "What's happening?"

I waited for Father Andrew to answer.

"The icon is weeping. Oh my gosh, I've never actually seen this

happen before." He looked at me. "Is this what the icons looked like . .
. the ones you saw in Chicago, and at the church near the monastery?"

"Yes. And can you smell the fragrance? It's myrrh—her tears
smell like roses!"

"Like Mare smelled in your book!" Nora said, and we smiled at
each other.

Mark hadn't said a word, but now he stepped closer to the icon.
"What is this? Some sort of trick? How do you know it's real?"

Father Andrew looked at Mark. "That's really an excellent
question, and at some point we should have a bishop come and
verify the event. To confirm that it is a miracle."

"A miracle, huh? Just because some liquid is leaking out of a
piece of wood? My daughter is lying in that bed dying and you talk
about miracles?"

Nora grabbed my arm. "Adele. Can Shelby be anointed with
these tears?" We both looked at Father Andrew.

"Yes. Let's do it now. We need some cotton."

I saw bandages in packages on a shelf and opened one of them.
Tearing off a piece of the cotton, I handed it to Father Andrew. He
looked at Mark and Nora.

"Do you want me to anoint your daughter?"

"Yes! Of course we do!" Nora almost shouted. Mark shook his
head and looked at the ground without a word.

Father Andrew dipped a piece of the cotton into the liquid in the
cup and approached Shelby. Touching the cotton to her forehead, he
made two strokes, making the sign of the cross, and said, "For the
healing of soul and body." He repeated this on her neck and both of
her hands. And then he turned back to the icon and prayed:

"We thy faithful servants, standing with compunction before
thy icon, do praise thee with songs, O Queen of All. Send down thy
healing upon thy servants who now run to thee, that we may joyfully
cry to thee: Rejoice, O Queen of All, who dost heal our infirmities
by thy grace."

"Father!" Nora cried out. "Look at Shelby! She's opening her eyes."

We all moved quickly to the bed, and Shelby opened her eyes wide, staring first at her mother and father, and then at Father Andrew and me. Nora pushed the call button by the bed and a nurse answered, "May I help you, Mrs. Richardson?"

"Yes! Shelby's eyes are open. Come in here, now!"

Within seconds a nurse arrived, followed by a man in a white coat.

"Dr. Wilson!" Nora stepped back so that the nurse and the doctor could both get close enough to Shelby to see what was happening.

Dr. Wilson looked at Shelby. "I'm going to pull this tube out now, okay? On the count of three I want you to blow out through your mouth."

Shelby coughed as he removed the tube, then she looked at her mother and said, "Mommy—what's happening? Am I back in the hospital?"

Nora and Mark reached for Shelby's hands, one on each side of her bed. "Yes, sweetheart. You had a relapse a few days ago. But something amazing just happened."

Shelby looked at me and then at Father Andrew in his black cassock and large silver pectoral cross. "Who—who are they?"

"This is Adele Covington, the author I told you about who spoke at the library recently. Remember? She told us about weeping icons."

"Hello, Shelby." I smiled, fighting back tears. "It's so wonderful to finally meet you."

"And this is Father Andrew." Nora motioned for him to come closer to the bed. "He was praying for you, and this icon of the Mother of God—well, it started weeping."

"Weeping? What do you mean? It's just a painting, right?" Shelby sat up to get a better view of the icon. Father Andrew spoke next.

"Hi, Shelby. You are right that icons are paintings, but they are much more than that. They are holy images, representing Christ,

His mother, and the saints. We offer prayers before them, and sometimes they are known to work miracles."

Shelby looked at her parents, and then back at Father Andrew. "Miracles? Like what?"

"Well, today I anointed you with the holy oil—which we call tears—from the icon, and then you woke up, for the first time in several days. I'm sure Dr. Wilson is going to take good care of you now."

Several more nurses and aides emerged, having heard about Shelby's awakening. Everyone was hugging and crying. It was like a spontaneous party. Dr. Wilson ordered tests to assess Shelby's condition.

"Is she in remission again, Dr. Wilson?" Nora asked.

"We'll know more after we get the results of the blood tests. And I've ordered an MRI. Meanwhile I suggest that we keep this quiet until we have some definitive answers. I wouldn't want to start rumors about a miracle and cause a stir in the hospital."

Father Andrew smiled and stood quietly by the icon.

"What should we do now—about the icon, I mean?" I asked Father Andrew.

"We'll wait until Dr. Wilson gives us the results of the tests. I've got to go to the church to prepare for tonight's services. Can you stay here with the icon? I'll come back later tonight."

"Is that all right with you, Nora?" I asked.

"Of course. We're happy to have you here!"

As he left, Father Andrew asked if I would watch the icon. "If the cup fills up with the tears, replace it with a new cup and save the tears. I'll bring a better container when I come back later tonight."

"Are you going to call the bishop?" I asked.

"Not yet. Not until I talk with Dr. Wilson again."

The next few hours seemed like an eternity. A nurse drew blood from Shelby and took it to the lab. I waited with Nora and Mark as orderlies came and took her to have an MRI. The icon continued to weep, and I replaced the small cup with a new one. From time to time as we waited, I turned to the icon and prayed. *Oh, please let Shelby be healed, or at least be in another remission.* In the meantime, she was sitting up, asking for something to eat as color returned to her skin.

Finally, around eight that evening, Dr. Wilson and Father Andrew returned at about the same time. Father Andrew brought a large container and replaced the plastic cup under the icon, pouring the tears from both cups into another container with a lid. When he was finished, Dr. Wilson addressed Nora.

"Nora, may I speak with you and Mark alone, please?"

"That's not necessary," Nora replied. "Whatever the news is, Shelby deserves to know, and, well, Adele and Father Andrew can hear whatever you have to say." Mark nodded, and Dr. Wilson continued.

"I—I'm not sure how to put this. Shelby's lab work and the MRI . . . they don't show any sign of the leukemia or any spread of the cancer in her body. Anywhere." He looked at Father Andrew before adding, "There's no medical explanation for this."

Shelby sat on the side of the bed. "What does this mean? Are you saying that I don't have cancer anymore?"

Dr. Wilson choked back tears. "Yes. That's what I'm saying. I've never seen anything like this in all my years at St. Jude. Sure, we've cured lots of patients, but none with your type of cancer, and certainly not this far advanced."

"So, it's a miracle?" Nora asked, looking at Father Andrew and then at the icon.

Dr. Wilson nodded at Father Andrew, and everyone in the room burst with exclamations of joy—hugging, crying, laughing. Shelby got out of bed and approached the icon.

"Is this a picture of Jesus's mother?"

Father Andrew joined her. "Yes. And we believe that those are her tears, coming from her eyes in the icon. I anointed you with those tears, and you woke up, and now you are well. Would you like to pray with me?"

Shelby looked at her parents. "Mommy? Daddy?"

Nora hurried to join her, but Mark stayed back. Shelby walked over to him and reached for his hand, and he joined her and her mother in front of the icon. Father Andrew opened his prayer book and approached the icon.

"We pray before Thine Icon, that Thou mightest truly live with us, O Sovereign Lady! Stretch out Thy hands, filled with healing and cures, O Joy of the sorrowful, Consolation in afflictions, that having speedily received miraculous help, we may glorify the Life-creating and Undivided Trinity, the Father and the Son and the Holy Spirit, unto the ages of ages. Amen."

Another tear fell from the icon.

STARKVILLE

Jeanne

Starkville is part of what's known as the Golden Triangle in northeast Mississippi, which includes Columbus and West Point. It's probably best known as home to Mississippi State University, my father's alma mater. Dad was a starting pitcher on the Bulldogs' baseball team in 1948, the first year they won the SEC championship. It's hard to believe that was seventy-one years ago.

As I drove into town I tried to imagine what life had been like in Starkville back then. My mother was at nearby Mississippi State College for Women—known as "the W"—in Columbus, just twenty-five miles away. The tales of their courtship in these towns entertained me in my teenage years when I first started dating. They talked about meeting between Starkville and Columbus at "the Crossroads," which today has become an industrial mega site.

The city of Starkville now thrives with culture as evidenced by the large turnout at the Friends of the Library's monthly meeting. There were probably fifty people milling around in the event room when I arrived, and chairs had been set up in rows with a center aisle. It felt more like an event at a major bookstore in a larger city than most of the Friends gatherings I had attended in smaller towns. An attractive middle-aged woman greeted me.

"Adele! So glad you made it. I'm Louise Armstrong. We've been emailing—I see you found us."

"Yes, it was an easy drive, thanks. I haven't been to Starkville in about forty-five years. Wow. It's really changed!"

"Sure has. Maybe you can join me for lunch after the meeting and I can show you around. A friend—one of our members—has expressed an interest in chatting with you, so I hope you've got time to eat with us."

"I'd love to."

Another woman approached, and Louise introduced us.

"Adele, this is Helen McWilliams. She's from the Book Mart. They're handling sales of your books today, so I'll let y'all get set up before the meeting starts."

This was the only library on my tour so far that had a local bookstore handling my book sales. Now I could just visit with folks and sign books and not have to handle the transactions myself. Once Helen and I finished getting her table set up, I joined Louise in the front of the room, where she introduced me. Finally, it was time for me to talk about my novel.

"I always like to ask a few questions before I begin, to get an idea of my readers' interests. First of all, how many of you are interested in art?"

A dozen or so people raised their hands.

"Great. Three diverse types of art are featured in the book, so I'll read excerpts from sections that focus on graffiti, abstract expressionism, and iconography."

I read the prologue in which the teenaged Mare, the protagonist, is throwing up graffiti. Next, I shared part of a scene in the office of her mentor at Savannah College of Art and Design, Elaine deKooning, the famous abstract expressionist painter. I ended with a scene from Mare's visit to a monastery in North Carolina to study iconography. The audience seemed especially interested in iconography, an ancient liturgical art form that is mainly familiar to Orthodox Christians and Catholics. But graffiti—uncommon in Mississippi, or in many non-urban areas in the South, for that matter—often stirs questions in these parts. One of the younger folks, a man in his twenties, wanted to know more about it.

"How did you decide to have the main character paint graffiti in a small town like Macon, Georgia?" he asked.

"Good question. I set that part of the book in Macon because Mercer University is there, so there would be a younger population. And I wanted Mare's early experience with art to be in Georgia, since she ends up with a scholarship to SCAD in Savannah."

A slim, attractive thirty-something woman asked, "Why did you decide for the three main characters to share the experience of being sexually abused as children?"

"Ah, someone who has read the book." A spattering of low laughter filled the room. "In the author's note at the end of the book I mention briefly that I was also sexually abused. Novels often contain elements of truth from the author's life. I wrote a memoir before deciding to turn to fiction to express some of the darker elements of my own life."

"Are you going to publish the memoir?" the woman asked.

"No. There were too many people and situations that I didn't want to go public with, so I decided to let those experiences inform a novel instead." I was accustomed to this question at readings, and I always wondered if something personal was behind them.

After the reading, I signed books and visited with several more people. The last person in line was the young woman who had asked about the sexual abuse.

"Hi, I'm Jeanne Watkins. Did Louise mention that I asked if I could join y'all for lunch?"

"Oh, yes. Nice to meet you, Jeanne. That would be great. I just need to settle up with Helen from Book Mart on the sales. I'll be ready in a few minutes."

I looked around for Louise and noticed that she was on her phone in the back of the room. She had a serious expression as she finished her call and approached my table.

"Adele, I'm so sorry, but I've had a family emergency and I'm not going to be able to join you for lunch."

"Oh, dear, I hope everything is all right."

"Yes, it's my mother. She's in a nursing home. She fell and might need surgery, so I'm going to head over and see about her now. Thanks so much for coming. I'm sure Jeanne can entertain you at lunch."

"Of course," Jeanne said. "Let me know if I can do anything for you."

We took Jeanne's car to lunch so that she could take me on a tour of the Cotton District, Starkville's famous new urbanism community. It was founded in 2000 by Dan Camp—developer, owner, and property manager of much of the area. It's a walkable neighborhood about halfway between the Mississippi State campus and downtown Starkville.

"It looks and feels like a little village in Europe, doesn't it?" Jeanne asked.

"And a lot like Harbor Town—my neighborhood on the Mississippi River in Memphis, which was modeled after Seaside, Florida," I said.

"Exactly. Look at these gorgeous Greek Revival mansions, and these little row houses. There are also lots of apartments, which are popular with the college kids. Oh, we're here."

Jeanne pulled onto a side street next to the Cotton District Grill, where we were having lunch.

"The crab cakes and spring rolls here are wonderful," she said as the waitress brought our menus. "But my favorite is the crab and macadamia nut wontons."

"Oh, my. Sounds scrumptious! You must not eat here often."

Jeanne flashed a quizzical look and I laughed.

"Because you're so slim!"

"Well, the crab cakes aren't too caloric, but I have to admit that the wontons are fried. Want to split an order?"

"Sure."

After the waitress took our order, Jeanne got quiet. We sipped our iced tea and she checked her text messages twice and furrowed her brow.

"Everything okay?" I asked.

"Oh, sorry. Yes. I mean, sort of. I'm a little worried about Louise's mother, but I'm also feeling guilty because I'm kind of glad she couldn't join us for lunch."

"Why is that?"

"I was hoping to talk with you alone. I've been following your blog for several years—long before your novel was published. And I read your essay a few years ago. You know, the one where you wrote about three days of binge eating and drinking?"

I nodded, surprised by her revelation. Just as she was about to continue, the waitress brought our food. Ironic, given the topic of conversation. We picked at the wontons, which tasted like sin, and I listened as she told me about her own issues with food and drink.

"I've struggled with eating disorders my whole life," she began. "Starting back in junior high school, when I began putting on some weight, like we all do in puberty, but I was panicked that I might get fat. So I started—" She stopped and looked at her food, and then continued. "Not to be too indelicate, I became bulimic."

Our eyes met and we both stopped eating, mid-bite.

"I thought you would understand, after I read that essay."

"Yeah. I definitely understand. I was also in junior high when my food issues started. My mother was always telling me not to eat certain things, that I would get fat. And in high school, when I actually gained some weight, she constantly told me I was fat. My eating disorder just got worse."

Jeanne nodded

"So, I'm curious, Jeanne. You read my essay several years ago. Why are you just now wanting to talk with me about it?"

"Well, when I read your novel and saw in your author's note that you had been sexually abused, I started to wonder about something."

"What's that?"

"I wondered if there's a connection . . . between the abuse and the eating." She put down her fork and pulled her napkin from her lap and dabbed her tears. I handed her a tissue from my purse before answering.

"I definitely think there's a connection. I was molested by my grandfather when I was only five. And again by someone else when I was in my twenties. But I didn't tell anyone until I was much older. At that point I was also struggling with alcohol. A therapist helped me understand the connection. I've been making slow progress over the years with my food and body issues. I did quit drinking, though—about six months ago. So, why are you asking about this?"

Jeanne cried harder and looked around the restaurant.

"Sorry. We shouldn't have come here. I usually see people I know. Could you come over to my house to talk some more?"

"Sure."

We paid the check and Jeanne drove me back to the library to get my car. Then I followed her to her house, only a few minutes away. She lived in a lovely Italianate home with a pale-pink stucco exterior, a gently sloping roof, and deep overhanging eaves supported by a row of decorative brackets. The windows were tall, slim, and rounded on top. A square cupola sat just above the roofline.

"This is gorgeous," I said as I got out of my car in her driveway. She moved two bicycles off the grass and into the garage. I smiled. "I was going to ask if you have children."

"Yes, I can never get them to put their bikes away. Aaron is ten and Quinn is eight. They get home from school in about an hour."

I looked at my watch. "Do you need to pick them up?"

"No, we carpool. A neighbor will drop them off today."

Inside I looked around while Jeanne put on a pot of coffee. Bookshelves were everywhere, overflowing with volumes of Southern literature, poetry, and medical journals. "What's with the medical books?" I asked.

"My husband is a physician. A pediatric surgeon, actually."

That explained the nice home for someone her age.

"I assume you're a stay-at-home mom?" I asked while looking at a large portrait over the fireplace in the den. Her husband and children were gorgeous, and she looked perfect. I thought about the lyrics to a Mary Chapin Carpenter song, "Every Christmas card showed a perfect family," and wondered what Jeanne had brought me here to tell me.

Jeanne joined me in the den when the coffee was ready, and we sat on the couch together. I waited for her to pick up the conversation where we left off at the restaurant.

"I've never told anyone about this. I played soccer starting when I was around six. By the time I was in junior high, I was on a competitive team. We traveled to lots of tournaments. My parents were divorced, and my mother worked full time. So, I usually went on those trips with other girls on the team and whichever of their parents was driving us. Sometimes our coach would take several of us in his van." She sipped her coffee and set it back on the table, closing her eyes.

"It's okay, Jeanne. Take your time," I said.

"So, it seemed innocent enough at first. He would pat me on the bottom after I scored a goal. And hold me in a tight hug at the end of a game. But one night when he drove us back to the hotel, as the other girls and I were hopping out of the van to head into the hotel, he stopped me, said he wanted to talk to me for a minute. Of course I thought it was just something about the game, so I went with him to his hotel room."

She covered her face with her hands before continuing.

"It all happened so fast. I trusted him so much. I didn't realize what he was doing until he had raped me. I was pretty naïve, so I didn't see it coming."

I scooted closer to her on the couch and put my arm around her.

"The thing is, it happened more than once. My father left when I was little, and he wasn't really in my life much, so Coach Andy was like the father I never had. I was confused and thought he really loved me."

"Of course you did. I thought my grandfather loved me. These men—these patriarchs who are supposed to protect us—we are so vulnerable to them."

"How did it end, with your grandfather? How did you make it stop?"

"He actually died when I was five, so it only happened a few times. But I've learned that any sexual abuse at all has dire consequences for the victim. I met the author Robert Goolrick at a reading at Square Books in Oxford a few years ago. He was reading from his memoir, *The End of the World As We Know It.* His father molested him once when he was about five. Decades later he is on medication and in therapy and he's still not okay. In his book he says that he will always be looking for what he calls 'the imagined beauty of a life I haven't lived.' That's what we do, Jeanne. We look for that love in food, or alcohol, or sometimes just surrounding ourselves with beautiful *things* to try to replace the love we didn't get."

Jeanne looked around the room. "Yes! I'm obsessed with this house, and with clothes and trying to be a perfect size two! But I never saw the connection between that and what happened with Coach Andy."

"So, when—and how—did it end, with your coach?"

"Fortunately, his family moved away at the end of my ninth-grade year. But the experience ruined soccer for me, so I quit the sport. My mother wondered why I quit something I so obviously loved, but I couldn't bring myself to tell her. So I just said I wanted to try something different. I was a cheerleader in high school—and later at Mississippi State."

"I did that, too. Not the soccer; it hadn't come to Mississippi yet when I was a kid. But I was a cheerleader. And later I taught aerobic dancing."

"I teach yoga. And I run about four miles a day. If I don't work out, I can't eat, or I can't eat without throwing up after."

"It was like that for me, too, when I was your age. I was teaching aerobics every day, but if I missed a day, I wouldn't eat. I was in my thirties, and although I only weighed about one hundred and fifteen pounds, I still thought I was fat."

"So, how did you get past all that? You seem so healthy today."

"Okay, so I'm sixty-seven years old and am a good thirty pounds over what I'd like to weigh, but I'm finally learning to love myself in a healthier way. I've started working out with a personal trainer at a gym near my house, and I use our elliptical machine at home for cardio. When I quit drinking, my craving for carbs and sweets went through the roof, but now I'm starting to get a handle on the eating. It's a lifelong journey."

"Wow. This makes me feel hopeful, but I don't know what to do next."

"Do you know of a good therapist in Starkville? That might be a good place to start. Maybe your husband knows someone."

Jeanne's face fell. "Oh, I can't imagine telling Bobby about this."

"Okay, I get that. But wouldn't he notice if you were seeing a therapist?"

"Not really. I take care of paying the bills, and I could even pay with cash if I need to. I guess I just need to find the right person for counseling."

"Or—" I stopped before finishing my thought.

"Or *what*?"

"Well, you could just sit with this for a while. Pray about it—if you're a spiritual person, that is. Let this connection sink in. Maybe do some reading. There's a book that came out about twenty years ago that explores sexual abuse and eating disorders. It's got chapters by over twenty contributors, all specialists in the field. I can send you a copy, or a link so you can order it online if you're interested. It might be a good place to start."

The back door opened and slammed shut and voices rang out. "Mom! We're home!" Jeanne's children came into the den and stopped in their tracks when they saw me.

"Hi, kids. This is my friend, Miss Adele. She's the author who spoke at the Friends of the Library meeting today. Adele, this is Quinn and Aaron."

Quinn looked like a mini-Jeanne, with a bouncy blond ponytail and tiny little body. Aaron was a strapping ten-year-old who hadn't quite lost his baby fat.

"Hello," I offered. "It's nice to meet you."

"Hi," Quinn said.

Aaron waved then walked towards the kitchen, saying over his shoulder, "What's for snacks, Mom? I've got soccer practice at five, and I'm starving."

"Sorry about that," Jeanne said to me.

"Oh, he's fine. Typical boy. I need to use your bathroom and then get on the road."

When I came out of the bathroom Aaron was chomping on a piece of leftover pizza and washing it down with a smoothie. Quinn was drinking a Diet Coke and working on her homework at the kitchen counter. The scene made me nostalgic for my own kids, grown and living in other states with children of their own now. But I couldn't help but wonder how Jeanne's issues were affecting her two blossoming "tweens" at this important stage of their lives. I was sad to leave them, and found myself wishing I lived nearby and could be a part of their lives.

Jeanne and I hugged goodbye at the door and promised to stay in touch. "You've got my email and cell phone number, so please don't hesitate to text or call me," I said as she walked me out to my car.

I didn't hear from Jeanne for a couple of months. The call came when I was walking down by the Mississippi River, a few blocks from my house. It was almost sunset, my favorite time of day. The last rays of the day pierced a group of gauze-like pink clouds across the water. I sat on a bench to watch the show as I answered Jeanne's call.

"Jeanne! Hi. It's so good to hear from you. What's going on?"

"Hi, Adele. Nice to hear your voice, too. Things are good— well, better in some ways. I'm calling because Aaron has a soccer tournament in Memphis next weekend and I was hoping we could get together."

"I'd love to. Do y'all need a place to stay?"

"Thanks, we're booked at a hotel out in Collierville so we'll be close to the Mike Rose soccer fields."

"Is the whole family coming?"

"No, just Aaron and me. Quinn is staying home with her dad. He's helping her with her science fair project, and she'd much rather be doing that than watching her brother play soccer." Jeanne sounded encouragingly upbeat.

"That sounds good. So, when and where do you want to get together?"

"The last game on Saturday is over around five thirty, and Aaron can go out to dinner with some of his teammates and their parents, so I'm free for a couple of hours early that evening. Is there somewhere you could meet me for dinner?"

"Sure, or if you don't mind the drive, my husband is out of town, so if you come to my house we could have some privacy."

"Oh, thank you. That will be perfect. Just text me your address."

"Will do. It's about a thirty-minute drive; just let me know when you leave the soccer fields. Can't wait to see you!"

"You, too. See you then."

I thought about Jeanne all week, and finally Saturday arrived. She was at my door at six sharp. We embraced and she came inside.

"Oh, wow, I love your house!" she said looking around. "And don't you look great in those skinny jeans! Have you lost weight? Not that you needed to! Oh, I'm just blabbering on here, sorry."

"You're fine, silly. And thanks. We love the house, and no on the weight loss—that's just the illusion the jeans give. But enough about me. How did Aaron's team do today?"

"They won two games, so they'll be playing again tomorrow morning, and either in the consolation or championship game tomorrow afternoon. Aaron played well and seems to be having a great time with his friends. Thanks for asking. Hey, can I use your bathroom? I'm a sweaty mess from being at the soccer fields all day."

I laughed. "I remember those days. All three of our kids played soccer, so I spent many hot days on those fields."

When Jeanne emerged I had a tray of raw veggies and low-fat Ranch dressing ready on the coffee table. I was working on a glass of Perrier sparkling water.

"Would you like a glass of wine, or some Perrier or a soft drink?" I offered.

"The wine sounds wonderful, thanks."

"I've got some snacks ready in the den, and I thought we'd just order out when we're ready for something more substantial. Don't you love Uber Eats?"

"Haven't heard of it. Isn't that the taxi service?"

"Oh, I forget you live in a small town. It's probably not there yet. They pick up food from any restaurant and deliver it to you. It's amazing. Anyway, I was thinking we might order from this new farm-to-table place in midtown. They've got lots of healthy options."

"Great. Of course there was nothing but junk food at the concessions at the soccer fields all day."

With dinner plans settled, I waited for Jeanne to take the conversation to another level. After a few bites of carrots and grape tomatoes, she gave me a half-smile with raised eyebrows. When she spoke, her voice was a little shaky.

"Well, there's good news and not-so-great news. Which do you want first?"

Our eyes met and I returned her smile. "Whatever you want to tell me. This is your story."

"Well, the good news is that I found a therapist in Starkville—one with some experience with sexual abuse and eating disorders, surprisingly. She does a lot of work with girls over at Mississippi State, where there seems to be a lot of pressure to be beautiful and thin. Just like it was when I was there fifteen years ago."

"And when I was at Ole Miss, almost fifty years ago," I said. "So, has she helped you?"

"Definitely. I'm getting that connection we talked about when you were in Starkville—between the abuse and the eating. And I'm learning to forgive Coach Andy and to quit blaming myself. I've started to let go of my need to numb my feelings with food, or alcohol." She pointed to her half-finished wine on the table.

"That sounds like good news, indeed. And you know there's no judgment here, so let me know if you want another glass of wine."

Jeanne shook her head. "I'm good. I've actually cut back on the wine, but I don't think I'm ready to give up alcohol altogether."

"And I certainly didn't mean to imply that you should," I added. "It was just something I needed to do myself. Our journeys are different. So, what's the bad news?"

"It's Quinn. You met her, remember?"

"Yes, she's precious. What's wrong?"

"Well, I had been noticing that she barely eats, and she only drinks Diet Cokes, and she weighs about forty-eight pounds. Average weight for a girl her height and age is fifty-seven."

"Have you taken her to a doctor?"

"Not yet. The thing is, when I talked with her about it a few weeks ago, she told me that she was afraid of getting fat. When I asked her what on earth made her think she would get fat, she said that I always talk about being fat and needing to exercise and not eat and all that. Oh my God, Adele, what have I done to her?"

"Okay, I understand your concern, but let's not jump the gun. It's a good thing that she talked to you about it, right?"

Jeanne nodded.

"And she doesn't seem to be bulimic, does she?"

"I don't think so. I've actually stood outside her bathroom door if she goes in there after a meal, which she rarely does, and I haven't heard anything."

"What does your therapist think about it?"

"I haven't told her yet. Quinn and I only just started talking about it a few days ago. Do you have any thoughts?"

"Hmm. Maybe. Does Quinn ever help you cook meals?"

"Not really. The truth is, I'm so OCD that I prefer doing things myself, so I can get it done more quickly and with less mess."

I laughed. "I'm just like that. My kids didn't cook with me, either. But I think it could be an important step in healing for you and Quinn."

"How do you mean?"

"Well, if you could find a way to make cooking—and eating—something fun that you do together, maybe it would help you both get a healthier attitude towards food and your bodies. Even tasting the food as you cook and maybe making cookies together could help."

"Whew," Jeanne sighed. "It does sound like a good idea. I'm just going to have to make a quantum shift in my approach to cooking and eating . . . and mothering!"

We ordered dinner and relaxed into the evening until Jeanne had to drive back out to the hotel in Collierville. As we said our goodbyes, I encouraged her to stay in touch, and she promised that she would.

A few weeks later, I found myself missing Jeanne. It was almost Easter, and my own children and grandchildren were many states away celebrating without me. Memories of dyeing Easter eggs and hiding them in the yard, going to church in the middle of the night, and having a barbeque picnic on Easter afternoon came flooding back to me as I prepared dinner for just my husband and me. I picked up the phone and called Jeanne.

She answered on the fourth ring. "Hello?"

I heard a loud noise in the background, and then someone laughing.

"Jeanne? Hi, this is Adele. What's that loud noise?"

"Oh, hi! Just a minute—Quinn! Watch the spatula . . . it's about to get caught in the mixer!" More laughter. "And save some of that icing for me!"

"What are y'all doing?" I asked.

"We're making icing for the sugar cookies we just baked. Oh my gosh, what a mess! There's cookie dough and food coloring and sprinkles everywhere!" There was a lilt to her voice I hadn't heard before.

"That sounds wonderful. *You* sound wonderful." I wished that Jeanne could see my smile.

"Hold on—I'm going outside on the patio for a minute. *There.* I just wanted to tell you how much your advice is helping me and Quinn. We're enjoying being together more than we ever have, and she's offering to help me cook dinner most nights now. Aaron even gets in there with us sometimes, when he's not at soccer."

"Oh, my heart is so happy!"

"Maybe you can come down for the Cotton District Arts Festival. We'd have a great time. I'll send you the date when I get back to my computer."

In the background I heard Aaron yelling, "Mom! Quinn's eating all the icing and we've still got a lot of cookies left to decorate!"

"Sounds like you've got your hands full. I'll let you go. Talk to you soon."

"Yes! Thanks for calling. I'll be in touch."

My husband finished his workout on the elliptical machine in my office and came into the kitchen to refill his water bottle. "What's for supper?" he asked.

"I was going to order out, but I think I've got what I need to make some stir fry and pasta. Want to help?"

He looked stunned. "Me, help you . . . *cook*?"

We had never cooked anything together in the kitchen except for bacon and eggs on Saturday mornings. He had offered to help plenty of times, but I'm such a control freak that I would just rather do most things myself. One time he mentioned that maybe we could take cooking lessons together, just for fun, after he retired. I had tried to imagine cooking with him as a fun activity, but my dysfunctional eating and distaste for cooking had buried those thoughts—until now.

"Sure. Why don't you pour yourself a glass of red wine and see if you can find some pasta in the pantry while I start washing the veggies. We can chop them up together."

He smiled and pulled a bottle of wine from the wine rack in the dining room. On the way back into the kitchen he called out to our Echo Dot, "Hey, Alexa, play 'Help' by the Beatles."

We danced around the kitchen cooking our first meal together and singing, "When I was younger so much younger than today, I never needed anybody's help in any way. But now those days are gone . . ."

WEST POINT

Crystal

With a population of 13,500, West Point has about 10,000 fewer residents than its sister cities in the Golden Triangle of northeast Mississippi—Starkville and its neighbor, Columbus, which are each home to about 23,000 people. West Point is located in the fertile black prairie region of the state. I loved driving through this rich farmland on my way into town.

Fields ploughed and ready for spring plantings were surrounded with rows of trees, separating one property from the next. Large farmhouses and small shacks dotted the landscape, and I imagined what kind of people lived in them. I stopped at a gas station and country store about ten miles outside the city limits, filled my tank, and was about to head inside the store for a Diet Coke. That's when I saw her.

She rode shotgun in a rusty pickup parked by the pump next to mine, glaring at me as I walked by. Her hair was dirty and stringy, her eyes hollow. A large man got out of the driver's seat and yelled, "Hey, stupid! Get your ass out of the truck and pump the gas. I gotta pee."

"I ain't got no money," the girl said.

"Just pump the damned gas, idiot. I'll pay for it inside."

She got out of the truck and began to fill it with gas. She looked to be around twelve but was so malnourished it was hard to tell her age. Her flimsy T-shirt didn't do much to hide her tiny, bare nipples. I approached her on my way into the store.

"Do you need some help, honey?"

She looked startled, and shook her head, barely looking up from the gas pump handle that she was squeezing with both hands.

"You know, there's a little notch in the handle there, so you don't have to keep squeezing it like that." I walked a little closer. "Do you want me to show you how?"

"I got it." She cut her eyes at me, and then looked in the direction of the store.

"So, is that your dad?" I nodded towards the store.

No response.

"Are you sure you're all right?"

"Just mind your own business, will you?"

The man walked back out of the store and came over to the truck. He took the pump handle from the girl and put his arm around her, squeezing her shoulder. Then his eyes shifted to me.

"Is there some reason you're bothering my little girl here?"

He reeked of alcohol and scratched his scruffy beard. His long, greasy hair hung from a ratty baseball cap. I couldn't see his eyes because he wore Oakleys, even though it was a cloudy day.

"I was just offering to help her with the pump," I said, staring straight into his sunglasses.

"We don't need no help." He squeezed the girl's shoulder again— harder this time—and said, "Get in the truck, girl."

As they pulled away, I grabbed a shot of the truck's license tag with my cell phone camera. When I went into the store I asked the clerk if she knew the man who had just been in there.

"Sure. He's in here all the time. Mean son of a bitch."

"What makes you say that?"

"The way he's always handling that girl. One time she came in here with a black eye. When I asked her how she got it, she said she hit it on a kitchen cabinet door, some crap like that."

"Have you ever called anyone to report this?"

"Not my place. Besides, he knows where I live. I don't want to get on that man's bad side."

I got my Diet Coke and continued into town, but it was hard to focus on anything but the girl. A tall windmill temporarily got my attention as I approached West Point's downtown area. I had read that the windmill was the unofficial symbol of the town.

In the 1970s, a cattle rancher erected one above a water well on Highway 50 east of town. West Point's famous Prairie Arts Festival adopted the windmill image as part of its logo. In 1992 the city of West Point, Nebraska, realized that there was another town with its name located on a fertile prairie, so they donated this second windmill to their Mississippi cousin. Looking at it gave me the feeling of being in the Midwest.

A few minutes later I arrived at the Bryan Public Library. A cheerful middle-aged woman at the front desk greeted me.

"You must be Miz Covington, our guest author! Welcome to West Point!"

"Thank you, but please call me Adele. Are you Thelma?"

"Yes. Did you have any trouble finding us?" She came out from behind the counter and directed me towards a hallway leading to the activity room.

"No, it was an easy drive. I love the scenery along the way—I don't see much farmland in Memphis." I thought about mentioning the girl at the gas station, but Thelma quickly ushered me into a room abuzz with ladies from the Friends group, and I decided it wasn't the time or place.

There is something strangely comforting about the similarities in these gatherings from one small town to another. For one thing, the library exteriors in West Point, Starkville, and Pontotoc look so much alike I wondered if they had been designed by the same architect. And the lunch menus seemed to be the standard fare—pimento cheese or chicken salad sandwiches on white bread with the crusts cut off, potato chips, and Jell-O salad. And of course sweet tea.

"No thank you," I said to the woman offering me the tea. I had brought my Diet Coke and hoped I hadn't offended anyone.

Once the fifteen or so people—this time all women—were seated, Thelma introduced me, and I addressed the group. After my tongue-in-cheek apologies for having gone to Ole Miss rather than Mississippi State, which was only twenty-one miles away, I began to talk about my novel. How many had read it? Three people raised their hands. The Friends groups often liked to meet an author and hear her speak before deciding whether or not to buy her book. So, my job was to sell them on my novel's entertainment or inspirational value.

One of the ladies was president of the arts council, so I decided to talk for a bit about the art featured in the book, especially the parts about abstract painting and Byzantine iconography. Another woman, a longtime member of Immaculate Conception Catholic Church, was interested in the scenes that took place in a Catholic church in the novel, as well as the part the Catholic priest played in the life of Mare, the young protagonist.

"Father Joseph was a kind and faithful priest," I was glad to say. "Unfortunately, not everyone in Mare's life was like him. She was abused by her own father before she escaped from the religious cult he led, and then again by her foster father."

I noticed one of the women in the back row dabbing at her eyes with a Kleenex and made a mental note to talk with her afterwards. It seems there are always folks at these events who are in pain and just looking for someone to talk to. Fortunately, she waited until everyone else had purchased books and had them signed before approaching.

"Hi, my name is Nadine. Nadine Montgomery."

"Hi, Nadine. I see you've already got a copy of my book. Would you like me to sign it for you?"

"Please." She didn't smile, and I sensed a deep sadness in her countenance.

"I couldn't help but notice that you were a bit emotional during my reading. What part of the book moved you the most?" I asked as I inscribed her copy.

"Well, the part where Mare was molested." She paused, and then added, "I couldn't help but wonder—"

"Wonder what?" I stopped writing and looked at Nadine's tears. "Oh, my goodness. Here, come and sit down." I pulled out a chair next to mine at the table.

"It's my daughter," she said, choking back sobs. "She was kidnapped about two years ago."

"Oh my gosh! Is she okay? What happened?"

Nadine shook her head.

"We were living in Columbus. I was teaching at the W and my husband was at the Air Force base. Crystal—that's our daughter—was walking with some friends in their neighborhood one day when this man in a pickup truck stopped and asked the girls if they needed a ride. Crystal's friends told us later that they broke out into a run, but when they looked back, they saw Crystal sitting in the cab of the truck as it pulled away."

"How old was she?"

"She was ten. We never worried about her when she was on the base, but I let her go home with a school friend who lived about ten minutes from their school. I never should have done that!"

Nadine lapsed into a full sob, and I looked around the room and found a box of Kleenex and brought them to our table. My mind was going a hundred miles an hour, but I proceeded slowly.

"So, was she ever found?"

"No. They searched the area for days, weeks, months. My

husband blamed me, and we fought about it for a year before our marriage broke up. Crystal was—*is*—our only child. I was devastated. Got so depressed I couldn't work, so the university had to lay me off."

"I can't imagine what you've been through. And I'm sorry if reading my novel brought back such painful memories."

"No—I mean, it's okay. I love to read, and I seem to be drawn to stories with a bit of darkness to them."

"Me too. I was molested by my grandfather when I was five. I wrote a memoir about how the abuse affected my life, but I decided not to publish it. I chose to use that experience to inspire a novel instead."

Thelma was cleaning up from lunch and saw that we were deep in conversation. She walked over to our table and offered us coffee.

"Thanks, that would be great," I said. Nadine nodded.

"So, how did you end up in West Point?" I asked.

"After my husband and I split up and I lost my job, I wanted to get away from Columbus, and all the memories. East Mississippi Community College was hiring, so I moved here about three months ago. Started teaching spring semester."

"Okay, Nadine, I'm going to tell you about something, but I don't want you to overreact. It's been bothering me since earlier today."

Thelma brought our coffee, and I asked her to join us at the table, thinking Nadine might need a friend to help her process what I was about to say. I told them about the girl in the pickup truck at the gas station out on Highway 45—and the man with her. And what the gas station attendant told me about the girl's black eye.

"How old was she?" Nadine's hand trembled, and she put her coffee cup down on the table.

"I would guess around twelve, but it's hard to say."

"Oh, God! Crystal would be twelve now. What color was her hair?"

"Kind of light brown, sandy-colored."

"So, where did they go? Did you see them drive away?"

"They took off going north on 45." I pulled my cell phone from my purse. "I took a picture of the license tag."

"We need to call the police. Now." Thelma was up from the table and yelling at a library employee, who came running into the room. The next few minutes were a flurry of phone calls—first to 911, then to the local sheriff, and finally Nadine said she needed to call her ex-husband.

The sheriff arrived within twenty minutes to interview me. *What color was the truck? What time were they at the gas station? Which way did they drive when they left? What did the man look like?* And then he left, and I stayed with Nadine and Thelma. Others had gathered with us at the library—some of the Friends group who had been there earlier, a coworker of Nadine's from the college, and finally her ex-husband arrived from Columbus in his fatigues.

"Where is she? The woman who saw the girl?" he shouted as he entered the room.

"This is her." Nadine motioned for him to join us at the table. "This is Adele."

"I'm Crystal's father, Charles Montgomery. How long ago did you see her?"

I looked at my watch. "It was about eleven thirty this morning, just before I got to town. Out on Highway 45."

Charles looked at Nadine. "Why are you just sitting there? Shouldn't we be doing something?"

Nadine stood so that they were face-to-face. "Your anger isn't going to help us find her, Charles. It never has."

His whole body seemed to cave in on itself, and he and Nadine fell into an embrace, both crying and shaking. After a minute Charles asked, "Where's the sheriff? Didn't you say he had been here?"

Thelma stepped in. "They've taken some men out to the Exxon

station on 45 to question the clerk there, the one who said she's seen the man and the girl before."

"I'm going out there!" Charles said.

"Oh, honey, please wait here with me. Sheriff Jackson said he'd let me know something as soon as possible." Nadine pulled Charles beside her. He put his head between his hands, resting his elbows on the table. The room fell silent, and then Nadine's phone rang.

"Hello? Sheriff Jackson? Yes. You found them? Is it Crystal? Do you have my baby? Is she okay?" Nadine nodded at Charles and smiled through her tears. "When? Okay—we're on our way."

"What did he say? Where is she?" Charles asked.

"They're taking her to the medical center. I told him we'd meet them there." She looked me and added, "Can you come with us?"

"Of course. I'll follow in my car."

When we pulled into the parking lot at North Mississippi Medical Center, there were red and blue lights blinking everywhere. An ambulance and two patrol cars were at the emergency entrance. As we hurried inside, Sheriff Jackson met us at the door.

"Where is she?" Nadine cried out.

"They're checking her out in the emergency room." And then he said to me, "Are you Mrs. Covington?"

"Yes."

"Why don't you wait out here with me for a few minutes and let them have some time alone with the girl."

"Sounds good."

We found two chairs in a quiet corner of the lobby and sat down.

"Where did you find them?" I asked.

"The girl at the gas station said she had seen the truck at an old shack just a little farther out 45. When we got there, the girl was outside—it looked like she was pulling weeds or something. We motioned to her to be quiet and waved her over to the squad car.

She hesitated for a minute, looking over at the shack, and then she ran towards us and fell into my arms. Two deputies and three men from the West Point Police surrounded the shack pretty quickly and called out to the man to come outside with his hands up. Next thing we knew he was blasting shots through the window. An ambulance pulled up about then and two paramedics coaxed the girl into the bus. I followed them here."

"Have you heard what happened after you left?"

"One of my deputies called me a few minutes ago. The man wouldn't surrender. They ended up shooting him. He's dead. Identified him from his driver's license as Leonard Abernathy. Was wanted over in Alabama for kidnapping and rape."

My mind went to a dark place. "Can we go back and see her now?" I asked.

He nodded, and we walked through the double doors and down the hall to the emergency room. Two deputies were posted outside her door, and Nadine and Charles were at her bedside. I recognized the girl right away, and the look on Nadine's face told me what I was about to ask.

"Oh, Adele. Thank you! This is our Crystal."

I smiled at the girl and she hung her head.

"It's okay, Crystal. I know you were just afraid earlier. I would have been, too. Sheriff Jackson told me how brave you were today when they found you."

Nadine hugged me. "Let's go out in the hall for a minute." She looked back at Crystal. "I'll be right outside the door, sweetie."

In the hallway I asked Nadine what the doctor had said.

"They're going to do some tests, but their initial report is that she's malnourished and dehydrated, but doesn't seem to be . . . *physically* harmed." Then she looked away and teared up. "Of course they haven't thoroughly examined her yet. They're bringing in a child psychologist to talk with her. It's the long-term effects of what she's been through that worry me the most."

I nodded, trying to think of something encouraging to say. "At least she's alive, and you have her back."

"Thanks to you!" Nadine hugged me again.

"I still can't believe this happened—that I saw them and then met you at the library on the same day. I know you and Charles have a lot to work out; he still lives on the base in Columbus, right?"

"Right. I don't want to go back there, and I can't imagine that Crystal feels safe either place—in Columbus where she was kidnapped or here where she's been kept like . . . like I don't know what for two years."

"Try to take it one day at a time. I've got to get on the road back to Memphis, but here's my card with my cell phone number on it— and Thelma has it if you lose this. Please stay in touch and let me know how Crystal is doing. And you and Charles."

We embraced once again, and I headed out the door of the hospital, into my car, and back out to Highway 45. After I passed the gas station, I looked for the shack, and there it was. I slowed down and saw a couple of patrol cars in the dirt driveway. And right next to them was a rusty pickup truck.

I didn't hear from Nadine for a couple of months, and I figured it was better not to bother her, although I often wondered how Crystal was doing. And whether or not Nadine and Charles had gotten back together. Then one day in the heat of the summer she called. We talked for over an hour, and she filled me in on everything that had happened since the day we found Crystal.

"Of course she had been raped, over and over. It took her several weeks before she would talk about it. And the man, Leonard, he starved her half to death, while using food stamps to feed himself. He rarely let her out of the house for the first year, until she was too afraid to disobey him and he would take her with him on errands at times—like to the gas station."

My worst fears were confirmed.

"How does she seem now? Is she eating and getting healthier? Talking to you?"

"She's put on a little weight, but she won't talk about what happened much. And she can't sleep. The doctor has her on some meds. We're really lucky to have the Sally Kate Winters Family Services in West Point. There's a home for children who have been abused and need a safe place. But there's also outpatient services. Crystal has been going there for several weeks now, and we're seeing some improvement."

"Is she living with you in West Point? What about Charles?"

"Yes, Crystal is with me. But she has awful nightmares. Charles and I are seeing a chaplain at the Air Force base for marriage counseling, and I think we're going to get back together. He can't leave the base, so it would mean that Crystal and I would move back to Columbus. She's not ready for that yet, so we're just taking it a day at a time."

"She's so lucky to have you. I know she's got a long journey ahead of her, but she's got two parents who love her. That's the main thing."

Back home in Memphis, I did some reading and learned that children who experience the kind of childhood trauma that Crystal lived through for two years often experience anxiety, depression, eating disorders, low self-worth, alcohol and drug abuse, and discomfort with physical contact. Some even become criminals. Physically abused children are also more likely to become teenage parents and not graduate high school.

Many victims of childhood sexual or physical abuse suffer from post-traumatic stress disorder (PTSD). Some even end up in abusive relationships and find themselves reenacting the past. I sure hoped that Crystal's parents could repair their marriage and work together to give their daughter the love and support she was going to need to heal. When I went to bed that night, I thanked God for whatever led me to stop at that gas station on Highway 45 outside of West Point, Mississippi.

PONTOTOC

Robert Earl

When we were at Ole Miss, my husband—who was my boyfriend back then—would drive thirty-two miles from Oxford to Pontotoc to shop at the Progressive Shoe Store. Founded in 1942, it was popular with folks all over the region, and catered to the guys at Ole Miss and Mississippi State. He drove there because he wears a size 13/14 AA, which is really hard to find. Progressive carries sizes up to 17, with widths from AA to EEEE. (Forty-eight years later, he still shops with them online!)

I never made the trip with him. In fact, I had never been to Pontotoc until one day in March 2018, when I made my eighth visit to a Friends of the Library group in another small Mississippi town.

My drive down Highway 78 from Memphis took me through the Holly Springs National Park, known for its bottomland hardwoods and other wetlands that provide habitat for resident and migratory wildlife. Everything was turning green as another winter receded and the sun shone through the tall trees. I rolled my window down and wished I had made time to really explore this natural treasure. With 155,000 acres, two lakes, hiking, horseback riding, swimming, canoeing, and bird-watching, there's something for everyone. I made a mental note to come back for a weekend away from the city.

As I drove into town and found Main Street, I experienced another moment of déjà vu. The Pontotoc Library fit the mold of two other libraries I had visited in Mississippi. I made another mental note to ask who the architect might be. All three had brick exteriors with elegant Roman arches along the front entryways.

For a town of fewer than 6,000 people, Pontotoc has a very active cultural life, including its library. I looked on its website before visiting, and saw photographs of many events for children, as well as the Friends' monthly author lunch. I was impressed that they were able to get so many well-known authors to travel to this small community in northeast Mississippi to speak to a group of mostly retired folks. When I asked if they had read certain popular authors' books, they often answered that they had not only read them, but that the author had visited the library. I had some big shoes to fill in the shoe capital of Mississippi.

When I first walked into the event room—thirty minutes ahead of schedule—I was impressed that so many people were already there, picking up plates of sandwiches and joining their friends at the rectangular tables that had been decorated green in honor of St. Patrick's Day, which was coming up. But I was more impressed to hear live music, and to see a man playing "The Tennessee Waltz" on a piano, which was set up in a corner of the room. He looked to be in his mid to late seventies, with snow-white hair, a ready smile, and an Ole Miss Rebels windbreaker.

I walked over and stood near the piano, and when the song ended, I introduced myself and complimented him on his keyboard skills. He flashed a killer smile and offered his hand. "Robert Earl Walker, so nice to meet you. Mmm, what's that perfume you're wearing?"

"Oh, it's Chanel Number 5. I've been a Coco fan for years."

"Well, you wear it well, along with that dress. Green is a good color for you. So many women today seem to only wear pants. It's nice to see someone dressing like a lady."

"Well, thanks. And thank *you* for the lovely music. Do you play at all the library luncheons?"

"Whenever I can. The ladies seem to like it."

I scanned the room, and indeed, there was only one other man at the luncheon.

"So, where are the men? Don't they read?" I teased Robert Earl.

He laughed. "Sure, but they're more likely to show up when we have a crime or mystery writer, or a book about war or baseball or such as that. The email about your reading mentioned art and religion, and the main character in your book is a young girl, right?"

I smiled. "I guess you're right. But we'll see what you and your buddy over there think after my reading. I'd love to chat with you some more."

The president of the Friends group introduced me, and I talked a little about the autobiographical aspects of my book I am often asked about, and also how helpful the Memphis library was with my research. Of course, I did a lot of research online, but the *real* books with images of graffiti and the works of the famous abstract expressionists inspired my writing early on.

Most of my audiences have been fascinated by the scenes involving graffiti, and quite a few are interested in hearing more about Elaine deKooning and abstract expressionism. But this group was more interested in the religious aspects of the novel. One man asked several questions about the Orthodox Church and monastery that featured so prominently in the book.

"Where is this Orthodox Church today? And what do they believe?" he asked.

Growing up in Mississippi, I also had never heard of this church until a group of spiritual expats from Campus Crusade and the Presbyterian Church started meeting in the first apartment my young husband and I rented, playing guitars, singing about Jesus, and studying ancient church history.

I gave a brief history—mentioning that for the first 1,000 years AD there was only one church, and in 1054 it split into West (Catholic) and East (Orthodox) in what is known as the Great Schism. Most folks in the US, and especially in the South, are more familiar with the denominations that sprang up 500 years later when the Protestant Reformation split the Western Church. The Orthodox Church has remained unified all these centuries, and part of the culture it has retained is its monastic presence and the liturgical art of iconography, also featured in the book.

After my talk, the gentleman who had been asking so many questions introduced himself as Ralph Wallace, a retired judge.

Robert Earl came up to get me to sign a book and teased me again. "See, us guys do read. Judge Wallace is a very well-read man, and it looks like you got him curious about religion."

I laughed. "What about you? What do you do when you're not playing the piano?"

"Not much. I play the organ at the Methodist church down the street. And sometimes I play keyboards with a group of geezers who got up a band a few years back to play at events for old people."

His humble spirit and warm smile told me there was more to his story. Just as I was about to ask another question, Judge Wallace patted Robert Earl on the shoulder.

"Get him to tell you about being in a band with Jim Weatherly, back in the '60s."

"What?" I gave Robert Earl an incredulous look. "Jim Weatherly, who wrote 'Midnight Train to Georgia'? *That* Jim Weatherly? I didn't know he was from Pontotoc."

"Yeah, we grew up together. Jim started writing songs when he was about twelve years old. Got together a band in high school. I played keyboard for a couple of years." His eyes got misty and I could tell the memories were getting to him.

"So what happened after high school?" I asked.

"Jim was a great athlete in addition to being a gifted songwriter. He ended up going to Ole Miss on a football scholarship. Was All-Southeastern Conference quarterback in 1964, I think it was. The Rebels were unbeaten and untied national champions in 1962, and SEC champions in 1962 and 1963."

"Wow. That was only six years before my freshman year at Ole Miss. I see your Ole Miss jacket—were you at school with him during those years?"

"Yep. And somehow Jim managed to keep a band together when he was playing ball. We called ourselves the Gordion Knot, and we played at gigs all around the South after graduation, until he moved to Los Angeles in 1966. Took most of the band with him."

"Did you go to LA with him?"

"No, that wasn't in the cards for me." He smiled and looked at the floor. "I could have gone, but the Lord had other plans for me."

"What he means," Judge Wallace jumped back in, "is that he fell in love with a preacher's daughter, and she wasn't a big fan of all that rock-n-roll music, or the lifestyle that went with it."

Robert Earl nodded. "That's true. My Dot Lee—her given name was Dorothy Lee—was a sweetheart, but she wasn't having any part of the music scene in California. I had to choose between her and following Jim as he chased his dreams. I never regretted my decision, but I do miss those days of making music with him."

"So, what did you do all those years after Jim left for LA?"

"Well, I married Dot Lee, of course. And I taught music at Ole Miss for forty years, while she stayed home with our three children. We loved Oxford, but I couldn't stay after she passed. Just too many memories in that town."

"Oh, I'm sorry. I didn't know—"

"It's okay. That was ten years ago. Cancer. I moved back to Pontotoc to be closer to our daughter and her kids. Mary Ann was born in Oxford, but her husband was from here."

"Makes sense. But something tells me you never really completely got rock and roll out of your system. Do you ever get to any music festivals?"

"Not much. Although I've thought about driving over to the Double Decker next month."

"That's in Oxford, right?"

"Yep. They always have several bands in for it, and this year they've got the Como Mamas coming. Those gals can take you to church with their music. In fact, they each grew up singing in church, and now they do a cappella spiritual songs that knock your socks off."

"Well, why don't you go over and enjoy their show?"

Robert Earl smiled. "I just might do that. I'm due for a vacation from playing the organ at church. Maybe I'll make a little road trip over to Oxford next month."

After I finished signing books and visiting with folks, I headed back to Memphis and couldn't quit thinking about Robert Earl, hoping he would make it over to the music festival in April. I had been thinking about going.

Double Decker weekend came up and my calendar was clear, so I drove down to Oxford on Friday afternoon. I wanted to go to the Thacker Mountain Radio show that night, and with 60,000 people predicted to attend the festival, I booked a room at a hotel near the square so I could walk to all the events and wouldn't have to worry about parking. After Thacker Mountain, I found my way through the crowds lining Lamar Avenue to the outdoor stage to hear the Delta Saints—a Nashville-based quintet known for their psychedelic flares and blues tendencies. It was there that I saw him.

Robert Earl stood on the balcony at Square Books looking down at the stage. I couldn't get his attention with all the noise, so I maneuvered through the crowd, into the bookstore, and upstairs to the balcony. As I came up behind him, I noticed that his arm was around the woman beside him.

"Robert Earl?" I had to almost shout to get his attention. He turned and looked surprised, and for a minute I thought maybe he didn't remember me.

"Adele?"

"Hi. I didn't have your cell or I would have let you know I was coming down. I wasn't sure if you would be here or not."

"Yes, thanks to your encouragement. Oh—this is Betsy Anderson. Betsy, this is Adele Covington. She's the author who spoke at the library last month. Remember I told you about her?"

Betsy nodded. "Nice to meet you!" She shouted to be heard over the music, which picked up just as we started talking.

"Maybe we can go somewhere quiet and talk after the show," Robert Earl said.

I nodded, and we stood at the railing and watched the light show and listened to the impressive guitar riffs and vocals from the Nashville group. It was a beautiful spring night and there was a nice breeze up there on the balcony. Of course it reminded me of so many other times I had been there, with fellow writers and students from workshops and friends who lived in Oxford or, like me, just got there as often as we could. It was a magical place, and especially on a spring weekend when the square was packed with art and music and locals and visitors gathered together to celebrate these elements of its culture that made it uniquely Mississippi.

Robert Earl, Betsy and I found our way downstairs before the Delta Saints' show was over, hoping to get a table somewhere on the square where we could talk. The lines outside all the bars and restaurants were long.

"You know, I only live a couple of blocks off the square," Betsy said. "Why don't y'all come to my house where it's quiet so we can talk."

"That would be great," I said, "if you're sure it's no trouble."

We walked north along the sidewalk on Lamar Avenue, away from the square and all the music. After about a block, we turned onto a side street.

"Here we are." Betsy led us up the driveway and into her cozy bungalow. She made me a cup of decaf while Robert Earl opened a bottle of wine for them, and we settled down in her den. Robert Earl seemed comfortable, as though he had been there before.

"So, how did you two meet?" I asked.

"Oh, we've known each other forever," Robert Earl began. "Betsy taught with me in the music department for many years." They exchanged a warm smile.

"But we were just friends," Betsy added, with a nervous laugh. "The four of us spent a lot of time together, before we both lost our spouses."

"Robert Earl told me about his wife passing . . . about ten years ago?" I asked.

"Yes, and then my husband died about two years after that. Robert Earl had already moved back to Pontotoc, so we haven't seen each other in a long time, until he called out of the blue about coming over for Double Decker." More smiles were exchanged, and I could tell there was some chemistry there.

We visited for about an hour, and then I said I needed to head back up the street to my hotel.

"Let me drive you," Robert Earl offered.

"Oh, you don't need to do that. It's just a couple of blocks from here. I got a room at the Graduate."

"Will we see you again tomorrow?" Betsy asked.

"The Como Mamas are on at eleven thirty in the morning." Robert Earl added.

"Yes, I'd really love to hear them. Maybe I'll see y'all there?"

"Sounds good," they said, almost in unison, and we all laughed.

We hugged goodbye and I headed down the street to my hotel. I could still hear the music coming from the square, where thousands of people—surely most of them much younger than I—were still enjoying the music of the night.

I packed up and checked out of the hotel the next morning, leaving my luggage in the car in the hotel parking lot before walking back down to the square for more music. I found the Como Mamas, and fell in love with their raw gospel sound. My favorite was "Come Out of the Wilderness," but I loved everything they sang. I looked around for Robert Earl and Betsy, but they never showed. I smiled to myself, thinking that maybe they had decided to spend the day alone.

Memphis soul singer Don Bryant was on at one thirty, so I stayed for his show before heading home. He released his first album in decades, *Don't Give Up On Love*. It was recorded in honor of his wife of forty-three years, the soul legend Ann Peebles. I kept thinking how much Robert Earl and Betsy would love his sound, but I never found them. I headed back to Memphis with a heart full of hope and a soul full of wonderful Southern music.

I didn't hear from Robert Earl over the next few days, so I finally gave him a call. "Hey, I missed seeing you and Betsy at the music venues on Saturday. The Como Mamas were terrific. And this guy from Memphis—Don Bryant—was there. You would have loved it. What happened?"

"I'm sorry. I should have called you. We were planning on being there, but we ended up with a surprise visit to the hospital on Saturday."

"Oh no! What happened?"

"Betsy had a heart attack. She's recovering at home now, but she spent a couple of days in the ICU and a couple more in rehab."

"Goodness. I'm so glad she's okay. Does she have children in Oxford, or someone to help take care of her?"

There was silence on the other end of the phone for a moment, and then Robert Earl answered, "She's got me."

I smiled so big I wondered if Robert Earl could feel my happy vibes through our cell phones.

"And I've got you to thank for that," he added.

"What do you mean?" I asked.

"If you hadn't encouraged me to come back to Oxford for the weekend, I never would have gotten together with Betsy."

"I'm so glad it worked out that way. Please let me know when she's up for visitors. I make it down to Oxford fairly often for literary events, so I'd love to see you both again."

After we hung up, I found myself thinking that Robert Earl and Betsy's late-life romance would make for a great Southern rock song.

VICKSBURG

Miss Mississippi

It had been over thirty years since I visited Vicksburg, a lovely historic Mississippi city of 30,000 on the banks of the mighty river. Only forty miles west of my hometown, Jackson, it was an easy trip to Vicksburg's Civil War memorial park and antebellum homes. Today's visit would include a bit of sightseeing before and after my meeting at the Warren County Library's Friends group.

In recent years the downtown has blossomed, with several streets of loft apartments, bars and restaurants with live entertainment, and cute boutiques. Every street corner seemed to be at the top or bottom of another hill, giving the town a storybook feel. I wished I had several days to take it all in.

The Old Courthouse Museum, built in 1858, was fascinating, its rooms packed with artifacts like the tie worn by Jefferson Davis at his inauguration as Confederate president, the trophy antlers won by the steamboat *Robert E. Lee* in an 1870 race, antebellum clothing, toys, Indian and pioneer implements, and an original teddy bear given to a local child by Theodore Roosevelt. I was lucky to have retired docent Gordon Cotton give me a tour. Gordon authored more than a dozen books, mostly about the history of Vicksburg, the South, and the Civil War. I could have listened to him all day, but I had a stop to make on historic Washington Street, near the dock where riverboats bring tourists several times a week.

Lorelei Books, which hosts author readings and welcomes lots of tourists from those riverboats I mentioned earlier, was hosting an autograph party for several contestants who were in town for the annual Miss Mississippi pageant. The pageant had been in the news because of its decision not to follow the Miss America pageant's new policy to eliminate the swimsuit segment of the competition. I often wondered how many of the contestants struggled with eating disorders or felt pressure to have cosmetic surgery.

The topic came up when I met a woman at the Friends of the Library meeting that afternoon. The head librarian, Martha McInnis, had reinvigorated the Friends group after a few years of dormancy. There were about a dozen or so folks—men and women—gathered for the meeting, and I immediately recognized two women I had seen earlier at an art gallery and gift shop near the bookstore.

"Hi, Louise!" I greeted one of the women—an artist who had worked on sets for the Miss Mississippi pageant for many years.

"Hello, Adele. You remember Janet, the gallery owner, from this morning?"

"Yes, hi, Janet. I'm so glad y'all have joined the Friends group. Martha told me she had been recruiting folks up and down Washington Avenue."

"Well, I've always been a reader, and I'm glad to see the group get started again," said Louise.

Martha interrupted to get the meeting started. After her introduction, I talked for a while about my novel. Aware of the artist and gallery owner in the group, I read an excerpt from the book about the main character's time studying art at Savannah College of Art and Design.

"Oh, we've got some pieces by SCAD students for sale in our shop," Janet said, and then blushed that she had blurted out what might sound like a promotion for her store.

"I'd love to see them," I said, and others in the group nodded, relieving any embarrassment Janet might have felt. The members of the community seemed to have such support for each other.

When I read a section from the book about the abuse suffered by one of the main characters, I noticed a woman who looked uncomfortable. She was slim, attractive, sixtyish and stylishly dressed, even on a hot June day in Mississippi. I made a mental note to talk with her after the meeting. I didn't have to wait too long, as she approached me after I finished signing books and most of the others had left.

"I'm Melinda Davis. I really enjoyed your talk today."

"Thanks, Melinda, It's nice to meet you."

"Do you have a few minutes to chat?"

"Sure. Let me grab a Diet Coke!" This was my go-to drink on any given day, but especially while visiting Vicksburg, where Coca Cola was first bottled. We found a quiet spot near the back of the room where we could talk. Melinda seemed nervous.

"Are you all right? You seem upset. I hope it wasn't something I said."

"Oh, no. Not at all. I was very interested in your talk. I read your novel when I learned that you would be speaking today. I can relate to all three women and their struggles with abuse." She looked down at the cup of coffee she held in her lap. I waited silently for her to continue. "But your book didn't talk about a common result of abuse, which is eating disorders."

I listened and nodded, still wanting to give Melinda time to say what she wanted to say. When she remained quiet and fumbled in her purse for a tissue, I answered.

"No, it really doesn't. But I understand that consequence, and I wrote about it in another book—a book about my relationship with my mother, who abused me verbally and emotionally, especially when I was young."

Melinda dabbed the tissue at the tears forming in her eyes. "What was that like for you?"

"Well, she told me I was fat, and she constantly watched everything I ate and criticized everything about my appearance, from the clothes I wore to my hairstyles. And although I was also sexually abused by my grandfather when I was five, I don't think that was as harmful to me as my mother's continual nagging and negative comments my whole life."

"That was my experience, too, only my mother took it even further. She put me in beauty pageants when I was a little girl, and into my teen and young adult years." Melinda looked away as she continued. "I was in the Miss Mississippi pageant back in 1978. Made it to the top ten, actually."

"Oh, wow! But that doesn't surprise me. You are a beautiful woman, Melinda."

"Thank you. But more to the point, I became anorexic during my teen years. I felt so much pressure to stay skinny. My talent was ballet, so there was that motivation in addition to the dreaded swimsuit competitions in all those pageants."

I searched for something hopeful to say. "You know, the Miss America pageant has done away with the swimsuit competition."

"Mississippi seems to be behind the curve when it comes to bucking long-established Southern traditions and the way women are treated. I've been trying to think of a way to lobby for this change in the Miss Mississippi pageant, but I haven't come up with anything yet."

"Good for you, Melinda. Is there anything I can do to help?"

"I really don't know. But I've got an extra ticket to the pageant tomorrow night. Would you like to go with me? My husband usually goes, but he's come down with a bug and doesn't want to get out. And because I was a finalist in a previous pageant, I've got VIP tickets to the after-party. It might afford an opportunity to meet some of the girls."

"Oh, my. I would love to. I think I can stay an extra day. Thank you. Here's my business card, which has my cell phone number. Just text me what time and where to meet you."

The next day I took time for more sightseeing. I had heard about the beautiful windows in the Church of the Holy Trinity, so that was my first stop. Built in the 1870s, the church's impressive exterior was striking—redbrick with a Belgian slate roof and a broad zigzag gable facing Monroe Street, where I parked. As majestic as the outside of the church is, it's the thirty-four stained-glass windows inside, given as memorials, that the church is known for. Six of the windows were created by Tiffany Studios in New York. There are only eleven Tiffany windows in all of Mississippi.

As eager as I was to learn about the difference in technique used by Louis Comfort Tiffany in these windows as compared with the others in the church, I was most interested in the tall windows on the front wall, which were dedicated to both Confederate and Union soldiers who died in Vicksburg in 1862 and 1863. There are four slim windows, each containing six geometric shapes, and one circular window above them with this motto: *To the dead who fell in battle at Vicksburg in the years 1862 and 1863*. This was the first gesture of reconciliation in the South after the Civil War, unlike the Tiffany glass window in Ventress Hall on the Ole Miss Campus, which commemorates the "University Grays"—the Ole Miss students who died fighting for the Confederacy in the Civil War.

All of this Southern history was very much on my mind when Melinda picked me up at my hotel to go to the pageant, which was held at the Vicksburg Convention Center on Mulberry Street. Our seats were close enough to the stage to actually see the contestants' expressions. I had never been to any kind of beauty—or as they prefer to call them, *scholarship*—pageant before. And as ambivalent as I felt about some aspects of the competition, I had to admit that I was excited to see it in person. What little girl growing up in Mississippi didn't dream of *being* a beauty queen at some point?

I remember standing in front of my bedroom mirror in my first two-piece swimsuit in the early 1960s fantasizing about it. But when my thighs expanded a little too much in high school, my mother's nagging increased, and my long history of bulimia started. The body and weight obsession followed me into my thirties, when I ran an aerobic dance studio in Jackson. Even when I weighed just 115 pounds, I could only see those thighs bulging out of my spandex outfits in the mirrors when I taught classes. Any day that I couldn't exercise, I wouldn't eat. Or if I ate, I often purged. I wondered how many of these slim, beautiful young women onstage in their bikinis and high heels had experienced the same thing, or maybe they were still living that nightmare.

The talent competition was fun to watch. My favorite performance was by Miss Amory, Molly May, who sang Jennifer Holliday's version of "I Am Changing" from the Broadway musical *Dream Girls*, and I thought her choice was perfect considering the changes at the national pageant.

The girls in their evening gowns were elegant. The impromptu questions made me nervous for the girls, who handled most of them with poise.

I was delighted that Asya Branch won and was crowned the new Miss Mississippi for 2018, setting her platform to help children of incarcerated parents. Her father has been in prison over half of her life. Asya attended my alma mater, Ole Miss. She was the winner of the swimsuit competition during a preliminary event the night before I got to Vicksburg. It was the second time she won the swimsuit competition—she also won it in 2016. Her short interview question during the final part of the pageant was, ironically, about her thoughts on discontinuing the swimsuit event. She said she had mixed feelings (I guess so, since she won it twice!) but understood that the pageant wanted to focus more on empowering women than objectifying them. I so wanted to ask her about this during the after-party.

"Asya, this is Adele Covington. She's an author who is in town for a book signing," Melinda introduced me as crowds pressed around us.

"So nice to meet you, Ms. Covington. Thanks for being here."

"Congratulations, Asya. I also went to school at Ole Miss, so I'm excited that you'll be representing our school all the way to the Miss America pageant!" I didn't feel comfortable initiating a hug, so I just smiled and continued. "I'm wondering if you might tell me a bit more about how you feel about the swimsuit competition being eliminated from the Miss America pageant. I know that was your short interview question, but I'm curious to know more."

Asya hesitated. "I'm actually a bit disappointed. I mean, it was a strength for me. But I understand that the pageant is trying to focus more on emphasizing empowering women. But for me, physical fitness is also part of that power."

It was difficult to discern whether her smile was genuine, but I really liked Asya. She was whisked away by reporters before I had a chance to say more.

Melinda introduced me to a few other contestants before encountering friends from her days in the pageant. Finally, it was time to leave. On the way back to my hotel, I asked why she keeps going to the pageant if she feels so strongly about how the emphasis on physical beauty can lead to eating disorders and bad self-esteem for girls and women.

"I'm not sure. Somehow I'm still drawn to all the glitz and glamour. But I'm also hopeful that pageants will move away from the more superficial aspects like physical beauty in the future. We'll see."

Back home in Tennessee the next week, I read that Memphis native and Ole Miss graduate Christine Williamson had been crowned Miss Tennessee at the pageant in Jackson. And guess what? She was also the winner of the swimsuit competition. Her response to hearing that it was done away with for the Miss America pageant? "It's bittersweet. I understand we have to eliminate it to get rid of outside perceptions of women being objectified."

She added that she never felt objectified, but that she learned more about fitness and nutrition by participating in pageants. She said in *The Commercial Appeal,* "Pageants teach women the importance of physical fitness, having confidence in public speaking and showcasing their talents. In addition, it's taught them the importance of failing graciously."

Failing graciously. Sounds like a lesson I should apply to my writing career. I made a mental note to remember this young woman's wise words the next time I got a rejection letter from a literary agent or publisher.

Williamson served as Tennessee's appointed congressional advocate and serves as a national Alzheimer's Association ambassador. I loved her involvement with this association, as I lost both my mother and my grandmother to this awful disease.

I also read that a contestant in the Miss Georgia pageant was a size fourteen and was speaking out against the swimsuit competition in Georgia's pageant, which it would do the following year. I wondered how changes in the state pageants might affect the national competition.

Miss America struck the swimsuit event, but in order to reach the grand stage, contestants in most state pageants must strut their stuff onstage in bikinis and heels. Will the state competitions that do away with the swimsuit competition be sending fewer anorexic candidates to Atlantic City? I guess we'll have to wait and see.

MERIDIAN

Gypsies, Orphans, and Ghosts

I n the 1950s, I spent a couple of weeks every summer with my grandmother in Meridian, Mississippi. She worked as a secretary in the tallest building in town, which changed hands and names several times. At one point it was known as Dixie Towers, a sweet, benign name for the sixteen-story art deco masterpiece originally known as the Threefoot Building. One summer when I was playing secretary in my grandmother's office, I wrote a poem, which included these lines:

> *I spent many hours,*
> *Many happy hours,*
> *Up in Dixie Towers.*

From 1890 until 1930, Meridian was the largest city in the state. Today it boasts the most historic buildings in any downtown area in Mississippi. The towering Threefoot Building anchors the business district, and would make a perfect location for a Ghostbusters movie. I always wondered why the tallest building in town was called "Threefoot." Turns out the building's German-Jewish immigrant developer named *Dreyfuss*—which means "threefoot" in German—Anglicized his name to Threefoot. It's currently empty of official tenants, but I learned about its most famous occupant on my visit to speak to the Friends of the Meridian-Lauderdale County Public Library. The original Carnegie Library now houses the Museum of Art, and the Friends meet in a conference room there.

Meridian was my mother's hometown, so the Friends group had invited me to speak to them about my memoir, *Tangles and Plaques: A Mother and Daughter Face Alzheimer's*. The group of book lovers—mostly folks in their fifties through seventies—listened intently as I read excerpts and later engaged them in a lively discussion about Alzheimer's and caregiving.

When the meeting was over, Rachel Peterson, the president of the Friends group, had hoped to take me to see Merrehope—the beautiful antebellum mansion that was spared during the Civil War. But it was closed that day.

"Maybe you can come back during the Christmas holidays," she offered. "The house is decorated with trees from around the world and it's gorgeous."

"Sounds lovely. But I've been hearing about the downtown ghost tours for years, so I'm excited that we're doing that instead."

"Well, there's actually a ghost at Merrehope, too," Rachel said. "Some people claim there are two there. And the house itself is amazing."

The art museum was only a few blocks from several historic locations on Twenty-Third Avenue. Rachel and I joined up with a group of tourists who were being treated to a "ghost tour" by a local expert. Dr. Jones guided us up Twenty-Third Avenue and around nearby blocks, telling stories of various hauntings in the ancient buildings. One of them—the Pigford Building—is said to be haunted by the apparition of a woman in an old-fashioned white dress. I remembered hanging out with Carol Pigford at Northwood Country Club back in the '50s and '60s when my father brought us over from Jackson so he could play in the club's annual invitational golf tournament every summer. Carol and I would swim in the club pool, and sometimes I went to her house and met some of her friends. Now I was curious about why her family's historic building was haunted.

"The spirit seems to have something against men," Dr. Jones began, "and has been known to throw objects around and slam doors when male employees enter the place. Sometimes she leaves costume jewelry around the building as gifts."

Our next stop was the Threefoot Building, and I was all ears.

"The building is being renovated right now, as you can see," Dr. Jones began.

"There are currently no tenants there, but workmen have heard a child's voice numerous times while working on the building. And at the end of the day, when they are back down here on the sidewalk, they've seen a little girl up in one of the windows."

"So, what's the story?" I asked.

"Well, back in 1915—just over a hundred years ago—a little girl was playing in the tower at the top of the building."

Everyone leaned back to look up at the building's tower as Dr. Jones spoke.

"She probably rode the elevator to the top and found an open window. Curiosity got the better of her, and she climbed out the window and fell sixteen stories to the ground."

"How did she get up there without a parent or someone knowing where she was?" I seemed to be the only person asking questions.

"Her body was never claimed, and people thought she was part of a tribe of Gypsies who had come to town for the burial of Kelly

Mitchell, Queen of the Gypsies. Over 20,000 people viewed the queen's body before the funeral—and 5,000 people attended her burial at Rose Hill Cemetery. So many people were at the funeral service at St. Paul Episcopal Church that many were turned away at the door. Some people think this little girl was possibly in that group, got lost from her family, and wandered around town until she found this building and went inside."

"That's awful," I said to Rachel as the group continued down the sidewalk to our next location. Rachel nodded. Her expression was serious. When the tour was over we ended up at Weidmann's, the oldest restaurant in Mississippi.

Rachel treated me to lunch. It seemed that everywhere we went I was surrounded by pieces of my own family's history. The restaurant was owned by Shorty McWilliams and his wife, Gloria (Weidmann), in the 1960s. Oddly enough, my mother was engaged to Shorty back in the 1940s, but when he was deployed in the war, she married my father instead. I was sharing this bit of small-world trivia with Rachel when I noticed that she didn't seem to be listening.

"Hey, is everything all right? You seem to be worlds away."

"Oh, sorry." She sipped her iced tea and spread peanut butter on her crackers—a traditional table condiment at Weidmann's since the Depression era. "I always get stirred up when I hear that story about the girl at the Threefoot Building."

"Really? Why's that?"

"It's a long story. Let's order lunch first."

I ordered Redfish Hannah and Rachel asked for Gloria's Special salad. The vegetable plates also looked good, but I had heard about the redfish and couldn't resist. It didn't disappoint. As we enjoyed lunch, I restarted our conversation.

"So, can you tell me what was so disturbing for you about the story of the young Gypsy girl?"

Rachel nodded as she swallowed a bite of salad.

"It's not something I talk about often," she began.

"Oh, then don't worry about it. I didn't mean to pry. If it's too personal, let's just talk about something else."

"No, it's okay. I just haven't thought about it recently. Well, that's not true; I think about it frequently."

Our eyes met and I reached across the table to touch her hand, offering encouragement to continue.

"You see, my mother was one of the children who came to town for the Gypsy Queen's funeral back in 1915. She was actually part of Queen Kelly's tribe. They were camped over in Coatopa, Alabama, when Queen Kelly died giving birth to her fifteenth child."

I quit chewing my redfish mid-bite, hardly believing what Rachel was telling me.

"When the tribe came to Meridian for the funeral, their appearance on the streets of this conservative Southern town wasn't always welcome. Some people think that the little girl who fell from the top of the Threefoot Building might have been kidnapped and taken up there against her will."

"Oh my goodness, Rachel. That's awful. Surely there was an investigation."

"Not really. Gypsies were considered second-class citizens, and the loss of one of 20,000 visitors from all over the country invading the quiet lives of the citizens of Meridian in 1915 wasn't something to be taken seriously—evidently. So, no one really knows who the girl was or what happened to her."

"Didn't you ask your mother about her?"

"Yes, I did. The girl was definitely one of her people, and they maintain a fierce loyalty to their tribe."

"What about you? I would have never known you were once a Gypsy."

Rachel smiled. "We actually prefer the term *Romani*. Most of us consider *gypsy* to be derogatory."

"Oh, I'm so sorry. I didn't know."

"Of course not."

As Rachel spoke, I noticed her exotic looks. Her nearly jet-black hair, pulled back in a low bun, was set off by large looped gold earrings. Her dress was a simple black shift, but she wore a large, colorful necklace and several rings on both hands. Her skin was dark, which I thought could merely be a Southern suntan. She was beautiful, even for her age, which I guessed was close to seventy.

"So, how is it your mother ended up settling in Meridian instead of moving on with her people after the funeral?"

"That's the hard part of the story. Mother got separated from her family after the service at the Episcopal church. She followed her best friend away from the crowds and into the streets of downtown. They were about six or eight years old. Somehow they got separated, and she never found her friend again. When she got back to the church, everyone had left for the cemetery. She sat on the steps of the church and waited for hours. Eventually the priest came back, but all the Romani had left town directly from the cemetery."

My mind spun as I imagined her connection to the little girl whose ghost haunts the Threefoot Building. My redfish had gotten cold by then, so I put down my fork and continued to listen.

"There was no way for the priest to contact my mother's family. This was a hundred years ago, and the Romani people moved around a lot. So, my mother was placed in the Masonic Children's Home, where she lived until she was eighteen. That was around 1930, just after the Depression hit and the economy tanked. But Meridian was still opening new businesses, and Mother got a job at the Temple Theater, working in the box office. That's where she met my father, when he came to buy tickets to a show. They got married and raised their family here. I know it sounds like a happy ending, and I have much to be thankful for, but I know that Mother suffered greatly from being separated from her own family and culture and growing up in an orphanage."

I pushed my plate aside and motioned for the waiter to remove my uneaten lunch.

"Would you ladies like to see a dessert menu?" he asked.

We both shook our heads.

"Just bring the check, please," Rachel said.

"Thanks so much for lunch. And for sharing your story. I don't know what to say. I have three adopted children, so I understand a bit of what it means when people you love have suffered the loss of their birth parents. What was your mother's life like after she got married?"

The waiter brought the bill to Rachel, and after she handed him a credit card she said, "Would you like to take a drive around town with me and talk some more? We could go to Rose Hill Cemetery, and I could show you where I grew up."

"Are you sure you have time? I'm taking up your entire day."

We drove out to the cemetery first. After seeing the graves of the Gypsy queen and king, which were covered with bottles of wine and lots of jewelry, we found my grandparents' graves. Tears filled my eyes as I knelt beside them. My heart swelled with love for my sweet grandmother, the one who sewed all of my clothes for the first thirteen or so years of my life—the one who took me with her to work in the Threefoot Building when I visited. And I spoke to my grandfather as I looked at his grave, telling him (again) that I had forgiven him for molesting me when I was a little girl.

Driving through old neighborhoods where Rachel showed me her family's first home, I was amazed at how close it was to my own mother's early childhood home. And my great-grandmother's house, which was right across the street from my mother's. The small grocery store that used to be on the corner—Culpepper's—had been leveled. A backhoe was still on the property, surrounded by leftover concrete foundation blocks and piles of red clay, which is common in the Meridian area.

Rachel and I stood quietly at each of these settings of our families' roots in Meridian, Mississippi, and then we embraced. It was hard to believe we had only met earlier that same day. Rachel broke the silence.

"It's so good to connect with someone who has a bit of a shared history. And maybe your next book will include some of my story, who knows?"

We both laughed, and I thought about the T-shirt I had seen online that said, *Careful, or you'll end up in my novel!*

Since I've been back home in Memphis, I've thought a lot about my visits to the Friends of the Library groups in all the small towns in my home state—and I wonder how my new friends are doing now. Francine and Odell. Charlotte. Avery. John and Mary Margaret. Shelby. Jeanne. Crystal. Robert Earl. Janet. Melinda. And Rachel.

I hope I'll make it back around to visit their libraries when my next book comes out. I'm sure there are more friends to be made and stories just waiting to be told.

ACKNOWLEDGMENTS
AND DISCLOSURE

"It begins with a character, usually, and once he stands up on his feet and begins to move, all I can do is trot along behind him with a paper and pencil trying to keep up long enough to put down what he says and does."

—William Faulkner

For years I listened to many authors talk about how their characters took on a life of their own. I thought those writers were all crazy. And I was pretty sure that Faulkner was crazy, since I wrote a term paper on *The Sound and the Fury* when I was a freshman at the University of Mississippi, doing my research at the Ole Miss library in Faulkner's hometown of Oxford. Years later, when I wrote my novel, I felt that I was in complete control of my characters' lives. I even outlined all the chapters and knew the ending before I began. All of that changed when I sat down to craft the stories in the book you are holding in your hands.

Once I got down the nonfiction elements of each story— bringing the history and setting of each small town and its library into full focus for my readers—I imagined the characters who would interact with Adele, the fictional author who spoke to them at each Friends of the Library meeting. Some of these characters were inspired by real people I met in each town, but most sprang from my imagination. They came to me as gifts from a muse. And now I must thank each one of them for what happened next—they did, indeed, take on lives of their own, and like Faulkner, I trotted along behind them trying to put down what they said and did. It was the most amazing experience (and the most fun) I've ever had writing, and this is my fifth book. Thank you for sharing your lives with me: Francine, Odelle, Charlotte, Avery, John, Mary Margaret, Shelby, Jeanne, Crystal, Robert Earl, Janet, Melinda, and Rachel.

Of course, this book wouldn't have happened at all if I hadn't been invited to speak to those library groups. Special thanks to those who welcomed me, organized the meetings, and served up Southern hospitality and often delicious lunches, including Fran Smith (Eupora), Jim Crosby (Aberdeen), Laura Beth Walker (Oxford), Melissa Wright (Senatobia), Caroline Barnett (Southaven), Sue Minchew (Starkville), Lucille Armstrong (West Point), and Judy McNece (Pontotoc). Many thanks to Kelle Barfield, owner of Lorelei Books in Vicksburg, who welcomed me for an event at her bookstore, while the library's Friends group was, well, regrouping. And finally, to Richelle Putnam, founder of the Mississippi Writers Guild, who welcomed me to speak at their annual meeting in Meridian, reawakening many ghosts and memories for me in my mother's hometown.

My early readers and writer friends who took time to give me honest feedback on the stories or write blurbs are the unsung heroes of this book. First, those who paved the way with their own short story collections: John Floyd, Jennifer Horne, Suzanne Hudson, Lee Martin, Ellen Morris Prewitt, Niles Reddick. And these writers of amazing literary prose in other genres: Cassandra King, River Jordan, Claire Fullerton, Jim Dees, Wendy Reed, Julie Cantrell, and Richelle Putnam. Jonathan Haupt, director of the Pat Conroy

Literary Center, and Kathy L. Murphy, founder of the Pulpwood Queens Book Clubs, have given this book their love and support in many ways.

Finally I offer great praise to my amazing publicist Shari Stauch, and to these terrific folks at Koehler Books: President and Publisher John Koehler for believing in my stories; Joe Coccaro, Vice President and Executive Editor for his wonderful editing skills; Hannah Woodlan, Associate Editor; and Kellie Emery, Senior Graphic Designer. Birthing a book is always a team effort, and I'm so thankful for this outstanding team!

DISCUSSION GUIDE

Susan Cushman invites you to use these discussion questions as a guide for your book club meeting. If you would like to connect with the author for a personal or Skype appearance with your club, email her at sjcushman@gmail.com.

1. As the author says in the author's note—"About Me"—at the beginning of the book, Adele often joins you, her readers, as more of an observer. At other times she gets more involved in her characters' lives, participating with them in their journeys and being personally affected by her relationship with them. Why do they unbosom so easily to her?

2. In Francine and Odell's story, set in Eupora, a homeless alcoholic man helps an elderly woman fulfill a dream of publishing a book that she gave up on earlier in her life. And of course Francine helps Odell by offering him a safe place to live and a reason to get sober. Do you think their story is believable? Did you feel hopeful for them as you read it?

3. In Charlotte's story, set in Aberdeen, what part did the community play in rescuing Charlotte from her abusive husband and helping her get on her feet with a job? Do you think this is a reflection of how things are in small towns compared with larger cities?

4. What did you think about the way that Avery, in "Oxford," dealt with being adopted by writing a futuristic novel with a similar story line? Were you surprised to learn that Julia was his birth mother? How early in the story did you see that coming?

5. In "Senatobia," John and Mary Margaret's story deals with two huge life events: a biracial couple's experience on a university campus in Mississippi in the 1960s, and the way in which Alzheimer's Disease affects them fifty years later. Which theme was strongest in this story? What did you think about their living situation while their spouses were in a nursing home with Alzheimer's?

6. How did you feel about Shelby's cancer being cured in "Southaven"? Was it her mother's faith, the prayers of the priest, or the oil from the weeping icon that healed her?

7. Eating disorders and sexual abuse are featured in Jeanne's story, set in Starkville. What did you think about the way Jeanne's eating disorder and obsession with weight affected her daughter? What themes did you find strongest as Jeanne sought help for herself and her family? Hope? Healing?

8. Crystal experienced long-term abuse—on top of the abduction—in her story set in West Point. Discuss how/why she suffered more from PTSD (post-traumatic stress disorder) as a result of this experience.

9. "Pontotoc" is filled with music and second chances at romance, as Robert Earl returns to Oxford and reunites with an old friend—Betsy—years after both of their spouses have died. What did you enjoy most about their story?

10. Adele stays involved with the people she meets in Vicksburg and seems personally interested in the historical and cultural elements of the Miss Mississippi pageant. The subject of eating disorders comes up again, this time with societal and parental pressures being involved. Why do you think Adele is so interested in this issue? How do you feel about the swimsuit competition in beauty pageants, or beauty pageants in general?

11. In the final story of the collection, Adele visits her own mother's hometown, Meridian, and befriends a beautiful older woman named Rachel. She learns the history of Rachel's mother, a young abandoned Gypsy girl whose kin haunts the building where Adele's grandmother worked in the 1950s and '60s. Does Rachel find a measure of peace from telling her story to Adele?

12. Which characters do you think had the strongest effect on Adele, and why?

13. Which stories elicited the strongest emotional response from you as a reader? Was it because you could relate to the issues facing the characters, such as domestic violence, caring for someone with Alzheimer's, eating disorders, or cancer and a miraculous healing?

14. If you could ask the author anything about the book, what would you ask her?

CPSIA information can be obtained
at www.ICGtesting.com
Printed in the USA
LVHW041535131019
633999LV00001B/4/P